THE *Listener*

THE *Listener*

DNA Designed to *Kill*

Ana Montgomery

outskirts
press

The Listener
DNA Designed to Kill
All Rights Reserved.
Copyright © 2024 Ana Montgomery
v2.0

This is a work of fiction. The events and characters described herein are imaginary and are not intended to refer to specific places or living persons. The opinions expressed in this manuscript are solely the opinions of the author and do not represent the opinions or thoughts of the publisher. The author has represented and warranted full ownership and/or legal right to publish all the materials in this book.

This book may not be reproduced, transmitted, or stored in whole or in part by any means, including graphic, electronic, or mechanical without the express written consent of the publisher except in the case of brief quotations embodied in critical articles and reviews.

Outskirts Press, Inc.
http://www.outskirtspress.com

ISBN: 978-1-9772-6778-8

Library of Congress Control Number: 2024905545

Cover Photo © 2024 www.gettyimages.com. All rights reserved - used with permission.

Outskirts Press and the "OP" logo are trademarks belonging to Outskirts Press, Inc.

PRINTED IN THE UNITED STATES OF AMERICA

Acknowledgments

I'm different, riddled with secrets, and thankful for everyone in my life who accepts that.

I want to give special thanks to Shaun Filion. Your almost daily encouragement kept me focused and moving forward. Your friendship is truly a gift, and I appreciate you more than you will ever know.

Huge thanks and shoutout to Detective Denny Deaton, Cincinnati, Ohio. It would be impossible for me to put into words how much I appreciate you and everything that you have contributed to the crime scenes in this book. There were nights that I would feel stuck in the powerless hole that is writers block and you would pull me out every single time. Your kind and fun loving spirit is unmatched and I'm so fortunate…. and incredibly thankful for you! Rock on Kid!

Dear Diary:

Another day of no remorse plagues me. It's haunting really. I'm not sure which aspect of this life I crave the most. Is it the hunt and the total destruction of human life, or is it the high of not getting caught? Literally, getting away with murder? Day after day I confess to only you as I know that you will keep my secrets safe. You are my listener, my trusted confidant. Do my confessions keep you awake at night? They shouldn't. They should keep *me* awake at night, but they don't. It would make most people feel like a monster. Somehow, I feel like this is just a part of who I am. Even though I'm a good person, evil lives in my soul. I'm not evil; the things I do are evil. With every life I take, I make the world a better place. I'm selective of my victims, and if I made the choice to eliminate them, it was an act of vigilante justice. They were not good people. Thank you for listening to me tonight. It helps having someone to talk to. No more dear diary, you are so much more than that to me. You're my listener. Until I kill again, good night, my friend.

Prologue

In and out of a restless sleep, I can hear the rain softly splashing against the windowpane. The wind carries a low howl as it whistles through the aging cracks in the sill. Trying to focus my blurry eyes, I gently shake my head side to side. A chilling fear is setting in as I feel paralyzed and unable to get out of bed. Soon after, my body will be shaking uncontrollably as the voices of my victims begin to whisper all around me. The number of voices is increasing by the day, but I can still single out and identify every single one of them. Some voice anger, some relief, but all are tormented souls. Most were bad people, and this is why I can't stop. I can't stop until I get caught. I have lost the ability to control my actions and the desire for blood and justice I now crave. Allow me to tell my story, to bleed on this paper, and confess to…well, murder. In a very methodical way, I will actually convince you that what I'm doing is right, because in my mind, it is.

Dear Listener,

I followed him again today. Watching from a distance his every move. This guy has no life whatsoever! Seriously, his routine never changes. It's all part of the game, the hunt, the thrill of it all. It's part of me convincing myself that the world would be a better place without him. I hate his name. I hate the way he talks and even the way he dresses. I loathe the sound of his voice. The way he talks down to nearly everyone. It makes my stomach churn. I can't get this over soon enough. Now that I've justified my motive, it's time to lure him in. A game of lust to trust with a delicate balance of sweet seduction. I prey on narcissists…they feel invincible until they fall for me. I'm a different kind of fate, deliciously dark, twisted fate disguised as a beautiful woman. I'll have him eating out of my hands in no time, and eating dirt shortly after.

A Brunch of Introductions

Every Tuesday morning the four of us get together for brunch. This is where we socialize as couples and celebrate our friendship. We are really more of a family. We live in Riverside, California, but we all grew up in the Midwest. Naturally, we gravitate to each other, creating a bond that is unbreakable. Both of our husbands work in law enforcement and are quite literally broken from the same mold. Hot, gorgeous, and both riddled with roid rage. Steroids are commonly used by members of law enforcement to maintain that stereotypical badass look. Despite the rage and total unpredictability when cycling on and off, they are very good husbands. I smile as I say that.

Let's get on with the introductions. I'm Heather and my husband's name is Michael. Mike has been with the LAPD for almost fifteen years. He's a great guy and we have the perfect marriage. The perfect life if I'm honest. We met and dated in high school, got married right after graduation, but never had children. We preferred more of a carefree life than most couples. Children would have been a challenge for us in that aspect. He is really all I have as far as family. I've grown to accept that over the years.

My best friend is Cassidy. Cassidy and I are real estate agents in Orange County. Two Midwestern girls both consumed and enamored by the everyday challenges of being creatively tossed into an LA lifestyle with very little desire to change. We handle it. I wouldn't say gracefully by any means, but we get through the day with a smile.

Tony is Cassidy's husband and Michael's best friend. We all graduated from the same high school and got married weeks apart. Clearly, the desire for adult responsibilities escaped all of us as they also made the decision to not have children.

This is a tiny snapshot of the organized chaos that is our life. Best friends and to my knowledge, I'm the only one with secrets. Is that even possible? We all have secrets and none of us carry the immunity of darkness. We hold them in as long as we can, but eventually everything that happens in the dark is exposed in the light. It's an undeniable fallacy of life that we all die with secrets.

Brunch

The continuous roar of laughter and delicious scent of maple syrup fill the air with sweetness. The Riverside Cafe is a weekly tradition for brunch. We spare no expense, on the decadent, in both calories and cost, spread. Drinks are plentiful and include a steady flow of bubbly, happiness-enriched champagne. It is definitely something we all look forward to every week. Recently, the dynamic has changed.

There have been multiple murders in the area, similarly executed and suspected to be the work of a serial killer. With Michael and Tony both working in law enforcement, tensions have been high. Copious amounts of overtime hours are certainly not helping.

Ting! Ting! Ting! Michael taps on the side of his champagne glass. We all perk up in attention, cheeks blushed and eyes slightly bloodshot from the alcohol-infused laughter.

"Happy Tuesday!" Michael exclaims with a flushed but serious look on his face.

"It's been quite a week, hasn't it?" He giggles and shakes

his head from side to side. "Okay, on a more serious note, I want to make sure that we all stay watchful and vigilant in the upcoming weeks. I know that you grow tired of me bringing this up, but we need to remain aware and extremely careful. This is definitely the work of a serial killer, and a very dangerous one for sure. Tony, would you like to add anything?"

Tony stands up and a troubled look wilts his chiseled face. "I'm deeply concerned too. Cassidy, I think it would be wise if you and Heather partner up for a while instead of showing homes alone. It's becoming more apparent every day that this monster targets no specific demographic. It's whatever is convenient at the time. That's what makes this so troubling and difficult to solve. Michael and I have discussed it in depth, and we both feel that it would be a good idea. What are your thoughts on this?"

Cassidy and I just look at each other. Neither of us wants to commit. Everything in our life right now is disrupted, and this is only going to add fuel to the fire. The last thing I want to do is commit to working together out of fear! Being the boldest and strongest of the two of us, I know I am going to have to be the one to step forward. With balls on fire, I have to fight this battle alone. "I really don't think any of this is necessary! I understand and appreciate the concern you both have for us, but…"

Before I can finish my thought, Michael harshly interrupts me. "This is not an option, Heather! This is for the safety of you both! Until we get closer to catching this guy, we have to be vigilant. Extremely vigilant!"

Wanting to calm everyone down, Cassidy reluctantly intercepts the conversation.

"Everyone take a deep breath and try to relax. We all know the depth of concern here. Heather and I will cooperate and do our part by staying vigilant, and if that means working together for a while, then that's what we will do. If nothing else, it will put your mind at ease. It's one less thing you will have to worry about! We can do that, can't we?" Waiting for Heather to agree, Cassidy sighs with frustration. "Heather, we can do this! Please, just for a short time. It's just until they get a handle on this situation! Can we at least try? It will mean so much to the guys if we do!"

I roll my eyes in frustration, but agree.

My dearest Listener,

His name is Jeff. I have been methodically working my way into his life for several weeks now, making eye contact and hanging on his every word. He's going to be so easy. Let's face it, he just wants to get into my pants. He wants a chance to prove his dominance to me. This is how I get him into my web. I lure him with mind-blowing sex. The kind of sex that leaves you totally emotionless and uncaring of everything around you. I have taken the lives of many this way. Why stop now? These men are trash and they're abusive, egotistical asses. This is what makes them so vulnerable; really, they just can't see it. Hormones are raging, egos are peaked, and they are riddled with roids. Makes for an easy target. I'm not a bad person. I'm seeking revenge for every woman out there who can't. The funny thing is, I don't feel any remorse or guilt. Now, that may make me a bad person, but not the act itself. It's my own spin on vigilante justice… I'm exhausted. I'm going to try my hardest to silence these voices in my head and get some rest. Thank you for listening…

Chapter One

My windshield wipers make an annoying squeak as they shift from side to side in an attempt to keep my view clear. Fog is setting in, making it difficult to see. The joys of winter on the coast of California, a little chilly for my liking and very damp.

It takes me twice as long, but I eventually make it safely to the gun range. Coming here has become almost a daily routine. I have to keep my skills sharp. Carefully, I walk in with my head held low, avoiding any eye contact in an attempt to go unnoticed. Across my shoulder is a red and tan bag hanging clearly unbalanced and containing more than a few unmarked automatic pistols. I don't really know the proper lingo, so by unmarked I mean that they don't contain a serial number. Several are Glocks that were converted to shoot multiple rounds with one pull of the trigger. Totally badass, but very illegal, so I always try to fly under the radar. I have trained way too hard to get caught or raise any red flags now.

Although I've made many friends here, I have never

actually told anyone my real name, for obvious reasons of course. I go by the alias Amy. It's simple and easy to remember. I can't be too careful. I find a cozy little spot in the corner of the range to get geared up. Safety goggles, gloves, and a good headset are my shooting essentials. I realized very early in my career that I needed to practice shooting with gloves on. It really is a learning curve more than a safety thing for me. It's necessary that I perfect my shooting skills while wearing gloves as I will be wearing them in the field.

Shooting is such a high for me. It's like a drug. I love the power I feel holding a gun in my hand and the pressure and release of pulling the trigger. It stimulates something deep inside of me. When I'm shooting at a target, I drift off into a deep, dark daydream. I pretend the target is one of my victims and I imagine the look on his face as every ounce of blood leaves his body. I watch him like a predator waiting for his kill to die. Patiently, I wait until his eyes roll back into his head, returning to the darkness as he gasps with fear and draws his last breath. It's an orgasmic experience for me. I think about all of these things as I look into the eyes of a carefully chosen life-size paper target. Mentally, I'm speaking to him. I pause and look into his eyes; my eyes are dark and evil, almost emotionless as I pull back gently on the trigger, releasing multiple

THE *Listener*

rounds without a single flinch of my body. No fear and no hesitation. Every round entering the death zone. I pause my breath as I step back and view the target. Absolute perfection.

"Amy!" I hear the shrill, high-pitched voice of my range friend. Nervously, I turn my head away to gain a little composure. With blushed red cheeks and watery eyes, I turn around to greet her.

"Michelle. Hey, how the hell have you been?"

I reach out with both arms to bring her in for a friendly hug. Michelle and I have been friends for several years, and we have attended several shooting competitions together. Oddly enough, we usually don't socialize outside of the range, and I'm not sure why. I think we would have fun together. We are both accomplished and effortlessly gorgeous! Sometimes I even get the feeling that she has a dark side, much like me. It's the occasional subtle hints she makes that I never comment on or entertain a deeper conversation of. Not commenting keeps me from accidentally saying something that I can't take back. She has stunning features, dark curly hair that frames her face perfectly while still allowing her chiseled, highlighted cheekbones to peek through. The darkness in her eyes is mysterious, with a hint of innocence. She carries herself well both in looks and confidence.

Michelle is deep in conversation with me, and I'm distracted and finding it extremely difficult to focus. In a dead stare I can feel my anxiety level rising.

"Amy?" she calls out to me with concern.

I shake my head a little bit from side to side before responding. "I'm sorry, Michelle. I got a little distracted." We both begin to giggle, and my cheeks are intensely blushing as the endorphins of embarrassment rage through my bloodstream.

"I'm not even going to ask you what you were thinking about!" Michelle exclaims. "What are you shooting today? Do you mind if I join you?"

I hesitate before answering, because honestly, I prefer to shoot alone. It's extremely difficult for me to enjoy the high of pretending to smell blood when someone is with me. But I also have a soft side, so it's not in my nature to blow anyone off. I politely act excited about her joining.

Michelle has a good aim and effortlessly hits the kill zone almost every single shot. It is obvious that she is a competitive shooter. Competitive, but honestly, no match for me. I've trained way too hard to let that happen! Michelle and I don't have an active social relationship outside of the sport of shooting, but within these four walls,

THE *Listener*

we connect on a different level.

Michelle is notorious for dating married men. Well, dating may be a loose term to describe her uncontrollable desire for a spell of romance. It's not that she doesn't want an exclusive relationship, but every man who has shown interest in her seems to be married. She is totally oblivious to the psychology behind all of this, but for me, it's classic! She's a beautiful girl and has worked extremely hard at keeping her shit together. She's spent hours and copious amounts of money on her hair and clothing. Although well into her forties, she has the smoking hot body of a woman half her age. This is what makes her a target for married men. He desires something taboo; he wants a whore in the bedroom. Meanwhile, at home he has an average at best, overweight wife who has never put any effort into herself. She is happy just being plain and unattractive to others. She's his Madonna, a plain Jane even he doesn't desire to have hot, unbridled sex with. She is for procreation only, the mother of his prized children and any other children born outside of this scenario will never exist to him. The men shower Michelle with love and make her feel wanted and desired, when in reality, they are filthy losers. Dirty, narcissistic bastards. And Michelle doesn't see this for what it is. She is brainwashed into believing that these men are stuck in a loveless, sexless marriage, and they turn to her for the love and support they are not receiving at home. Essentially, making her their savior. Sadly, she has always been willing to fall into this role in hopes of finding her happily ever after.

"Great shooting today!" Michelle exclaims as she grabs my hand and briskly pulls me in for a hug. "Hey, would you like to grab some dinner and drinks? I feel like we always enjoy our conversations while we're here; wouldn't it be more fun with some wine involved?"

I hesitate but only for a moment. I think it would be fun to take our friendship outside of the range. God knows I could use a drink. This is risky but something I really want to do.

"I would absolutely love to go out tonight!"

I discreetly pack up my guns and proceed casually to the front door. I am a little bit nervous and I fear that it will show. A couple of glasses of wine will help, but until then I will appear anxious. The closer I get to the door, the faster I begin to walk. I just want to get out of here as fast as I can. The last thing I want to do is toss out another mindless opportunity to have a casual chat by making eye contact with someone. I feel a sense of relief as I reach up and grab the door handle. A gust of very cold air hits my face and sends chills up and down my spine. Wispy

THE *Listener*

strands of highlighted hair temporarily block my vision as I push my way through the door. The two of us run as fast as we can to our cars, and off we go to warm up over drinks and pretend that we are shrinks.

I pull out into the street behind Michelle and follow her swerving car to the restaurant. No exaggeration, she was all over the road. When we enter the parking lot, she briskly and erratically pulls crookedly into a parking space.

"Michelle!" I shout as I slammed my car door shut. "What in the world was happening just now? You were literally all over the road! Are you feeling okay? We haven't even started drinking yet!" I am laughing as I say it, but serious as a heart attack.

Michelle steps out of the car, her eyes red and filled with tears.

"It's him, the guy I've been seeing. He is such an asshole! I hate the way he treats me! We can't have a simple conversation without him making me feel small. He has destroyed my self-esteem and self-worth. I simply called him to tell him that you and I were stopping for dinner and drinks, and he started harassing me about my weight. He's a total loser and I'm really starting to hate him for it!"

Seeing her like this breaks my heart. It takes everything within me to stay calm and not react.

"I'm so sorry he treats you this way! You deserve so much better. You nailed it, though. Jeff is a total asshole!"

Michelle stops in her tracks, turns around briskly, and with a confused look, she asks, "How did you know his name was Jeff?"

My dearest Listener,

I had a close call tonight. This is exactly why I don't socialize with people. Michelle was very quick to pick up on the fact that I knew his name. I handled it well. I think I did anyway. I will have to change up my timeline a bit. I don't want to do anything to raise any suspicion so I will have to cool my jets and wait a little while before making my move. I do feel a little guilty having an intimate affair with him knowing how much she loves him. Unfortunately, it's the only way to lure him into my web and gain his trust. I have observed his cruelty toward her at various social events and shooting competitions that we were both attending. He is a total dick. I will have zero guilt when this is all over. He is a bad person, and this is the only way. She will never leave him, and the abuse will only get worse. Remember, my friend, I'm making the world a better place.

Chapter Two

A chilly morning keeps Michael and me in bed for an extended amount of time. We are snuggling, making love, and touching toes in an effort to stay warm. We have been this close since the day we first met, and the flame has been burning hot ever since. Our souls are without a doubt connected, and nothing will ever tear us apart. When we first met, I never imagined that I would be where I am today. I couldn't see past being a housewife, a stay-at-home role model for my other married friends. Over the years my taste for life changed, and I've developed a lust for success. That's when I started dabbling in real estate, which ended up being one of the best decisions of my life. I needed to feel accomplished and valuable. I wanted more.

The sun is peeking brightly through the curtains, intensely warming the room, which feels amazing. The day is quickly drifting away, and it is time to get dressed and make the most of what is left of it. Mornings like this are what have kept our relationship strong over the years. I look forward to them.

THE *Listener*

We head downstairs, both desperately seeking a big cup of black, bold coffee. I can feel the tension beginning to build as Michael tries to find an easy way to ask if Cassidy and I have been working together. The truth is, we haven't. I'm not opposed to it, but Cassidy seems to always have an excuse. Things just keep coming up, and our schedules can't come together. I know how important this is to him, so I really don't want to tell him the truth. I don't want him to worry; there is no reason for that. I'm extremely careful when I work.

"How's your coffee?" I finally break the ice.

"Amazing!" Michael exclaims. "It's so good, I think I'll have another cup. Can I interest you in another?"

"I would love one, thanks."

"Heather, how are things going at work? I don't want to ruin our morning having this conversation, but I have to know. Are you being careful? Please tell me that you and Cassidy have been working together. It's been a couple of weeks; he's been silent, but I feel like time is running out. He will kill again! We just can't seem to get a handle on this guy. His pattern is so erratic."

"Michael!" I interrupt him mid-sentence. "How do you know it's a man? How can you be sure of that, and how do you know he will kill again?"

Visibly irritated over my question, he pauses and pulls

himself together before answering.

"Well, we don't know that for sure. We have been working tirelessly for answers. There simply are none! Whoever this killer is, he operates on a professional level. It's definitely not his first rodeo. Things are too clean, well planned, and perfectly executed. I'm just asking you to be careful! I love you and I don't want anything to happen to you."

I can see the concern all over his face. It is easier to lie than to tell the truth. Cassidy and I really do need to make the effort to work together more. It will make everyone feel better about the situation.

"I have to go to work now." Michael kisses me on the cheek and says goodbye.

I pick up the phone immediately and call Cassidy. Three or four phone calls and two hours later, still no answer. I send multiple text messages with no response, and in a panic, I grab my purse and drive over to her house. I know Tony will be working because he and Michael always work together. My heart is racing and my mind will not rest. Cassidy always answers her phone when I call. As I approach the house I can see her car in the driveway. I am a little relieved that she was home. Still, I'm thinking of the worst-case scenario. There has to be a reason she is not responding to my phone calls. I pull into the driveway and quickly jump out of the car. As I approach the door,

I glance into the side kitchen window just as she notices me. Her smiling face brings such relief. She pulls the door open, and I practically jump into her arms.

"Goddammit, Cassidy, why are you not answering my calls or text messages? I've been trying to reach you all morning. What the fuck?"

Cassidy's eyes get big and teary. I can tell immediately that something is wrong.

"It's Tony!" she whispers as we make our way over to the living room sofa to sit and talk. "We had a huge argument this morning. He was so pissed when he left to go to work. I don't know exactly what happened! It just spun out of control so quickly. I lost my cell phone last night. That's really what started this whole argument. I have no idea where I left it, and he wouldn't accept that!"

"Cassidy, how can you not remember where you left your cell phone?" I ask sternly.

Cassidy has always been a little squirrely and unorganized, but she is always attached to that damn phone. She stands by the fact that she has no idea where she lost it. I find that extremely difficult to believe. She looks a little rough this morning. I guess part of that could be the stress of the argument. I can see where Tony would be mad over this. Why can't she trace her steps back as little as twenty-four hours ago? What is she hiding?

"Hey, has Tony mentioned or asked if we were working together? Michael brought it up at breakfast this morning, and I told him we were. I wanted to make sure our stories matched. I think it would be a good idea that we start."

Cassidy quickly replies, "Tony hasn't mentioned it again, but I do agree that we should. Honestly, I've been a little worried. I will make more of an effort to work together if you will. It's for the best. I'm showing the beach house in Malibu today. Do you want to come?"

I can't say "hell, yeah" fast enough. I love Malibu and sushi, and we can't do one without the other.

Deep in thought, I sit outside on the patio and wait patiently for Cassidy to get dressed. It is a little chilly, but the warmth of the sun makes it more tolerable. The days are getting shorter as the fall and winter seasons quickly approach. I really don't love this time of year because of the weather. I love it for the holidays. Colder weather also means pumpkin spice time. Everything from coffee to desserts is riddled with pumpkin spice and I absolutely love it! There's also something very mysterious and cynical about the seasons changing, especially transitioning to fall. Fall is when everything dies. Homicides trend upward, and wickedness seems to have no boundaries. I shake my

THE *Listener*

head from side to side in an effort to rid my mind of these thoughts that are always tormenting me. It's funny how quickly my mind goes dark. It's terrifying really.

I can hear the hustle and bustle of Cassidy's footsteps as she makes her way downstairs. She must finally be ready. I stand up from the chair I am sitting in and head toward the door.

Cassidy stands tall in the middle of the kitchen, almost in a pose. "Do I look okay?" she asks with the cutest grin.

"You look amazing! Let's head to Malibu and sell a house! Sushi for dinner tonight?"

We both nod in agreement!

I'm going to have to side with Tony on the phone issue. Her story just doesn't seem to add up, and when I asked her about it, she quickly changed the subject. It's so strange and definitely out of character for her, but who am I to judge? My life is all over the place. I've had to lie constantly to Michael just to keep the peace about my work schedule. I don't really know what's going on with her, but as long as she's safe, I will consider it none of my business.

Selling homes in Malibu is an easy task, and honestly, there's no place on earth quite like it. It is truly the diamond of the West Coast. We arrive twenty minutes before the prospective buyers to open up the house and fluff things up a little bit. Everyone seems to love the flow of a fresh beach breeze and the smell of salty air. We add the ambiance of low classical music and an offering of wine and cheese. We always take into consideration the time of day when showing a beach house. In my experience, a sunset showing is the most successful. We are exquisitely selling the sunset. It is magical.

Confident that we sealed the deal, we close up the house and head over for some sushi and cocktails.

"Heather!" Cassidy exclaims while raising her glass high into the air.

"Cheers to us, my friend! We are definitely a dream team!"

"We certainly are!" I reply.

Our glasses come together with a high-pitched note. Our much-needed celebration of friendship and success lasts for hours, but it never really seems long enough.

Chapter Three

A gentle vibration on my wrist wakes me up from a dead sleep. A 2 a.m. wake-up call, it's go time. I've watched Jeff for weeks now, documenting his every move. It's been pretty easy actually; his schedule seems to be routine, which makes things incredibly easy for me. I carefully roll over and glance up at Michael to make sure that he's asleep. He's been working double shifts, so I know that he will be extremely tired tonight. I carefully crawl out of bed and leave our bedroom to get dressed. The house is cold and quiet. I tiptoe downstairs, grab my bag, and head out the door. I purposefully left the car outside of the garage so that I wouldn't have to open and close the door. The moon is full, and a thick layer of fog hovers over the ground. As I slowly back the car out of the driveway, I keep my eyes on the house, making sure I don't see any signs of motion. At a very slow speed, I creep up the road until I get the car far enough away from the house to hit the gas.

This is far from my first rodeo, yet I still feel a little bit nervous. Actually, I'm not really sure if it's nervousness or excitement. Over the years this emotion has been a little blurred for me. Whatever it is, it releases a high of endorphins that puts me into absolute beast mode. Nothing can stop me at this point. As I approach Jeff's driveway, I turn off the lights and coast up a side street. I sit watching and waiting for his arrival. He will be coming home from work at any moment. I need to be ready. Dressed all in black, including a full face mask and leather gloves, I inch my way, almost crawling, to the side of the porch, completely hidden. My breath is shallow and my heart is beating with vengeance. Inside my gloves my hands are sweating, making the gloves tight, hot, and uncomfortable. I glance up and see his headlights pulling aggressively into the driveway. Out of the car he bounces with an unexpected surprise. Someone is with him. *Goddamn!* I scream in the boundaries of my psyche. *What kind of fuckery is this? The kind I have to deal with, and quickly!* I grab my Glock from my side and with a slow methodical approach, I shoot her point blank, execution style. I can feel my heart beat high up in my throat and the acidic taste of bile is making me gag. She doesn't deserve any of this. Silently, I mumble a quick prayer that my response time was quick enough that she didn't feel any pain or fear. Jeff runs toward me and lunges at me with fury. He doesn't stand a chance.

THE *Listener*

Knowing that I want him to suffer before dying, I lift my hand and pull the trigger aiming directly for the left side of his chest, avoiding the kill zone. Penetration at his lung base will buy me the time that I need to whisper his sins as I stand over his near lifeless body. It's important to me that he understands exactly why I'm doing this. I can smell the fear in his blood and it is delicious. I whisper to him every detail about everyone in his life who he has hurt. His eyes are dazed and getting weak. I drag my fingers slowly over his chest, allowing him to feel the pain that he so desperately deserves. I bring my blood-drenched fingers to my lips and make him watch as I taste it. The metallic taste of sweet revenge. From my lips, with blood still on my hands, I bend down and paint a heart on the pavement next to his body. He is shaking with very little fight left in him, and I scream his name three times.

"Jeff! Jeff! Jeff! You deserve this, you deserve to feel the pain that you have inflicted emotionally on so many others. Who was with you tonight? She didn't deserve any of this. Who was she?" I shout with vicious anger.

"Michelle," he whispers as I watch every ounce of life leave his body.

"Michelle!" I exclaim in regret. "Oh my God! .She was my friend."

My dearest Listener,

I watched with intent as her blood slowly creeped down the slope of the driveway, partially seeping into the crevices surrounding it. Tonight was an epic fail. I never expected Michelle to be with him. I did this all for her, for the pain that he put her through. This was the ultimate win for him; if he had to pay penance, he would take her with him to punish her one last time. Hopefully, she went quickly and didn't even realize what was happening. She was my friend. I never meant to hurt her. I reached down and I closed her eyes with both hands. Her blood I did not taste, as her life was taken in vain. I whispered as I closed her eyes, "I did this all for you."

Chapter Four

Every media outlet in Los Angeles is exploding with the news. Confusion is sweeping the already-on-edge city, terrorizing the people by raising the possibility of a copycat serial killer. My stomach is sick, and hiding my emotions is proving to be more difficult by the moment.

"Heather!" Michael shouts, trying to get my attention and out of a daze.

I jump up quickly and twist my neck wrong. While grabbing my neck and reeling in pain, I angrily reply, "What the hell, Michael? Why would you shout and startle me like that? Oh, my neck!"

Michael walks over and reaches out for me.

"I'm sorry, babe, but I called your name twice before I shouted, and you didn't even acknowledge that I was in the room. I was a little freaked out! I'm just on edge. I'm so sorry that I hurt you. Three homicides last night had the same calling card. This serial killer is making a joke out of this entire city!"

Complete confusion covers my face, and I can't control my reaction.

"Three? Michael, are you sure this is the same killer?"

I can't wrap my head around any of this—three with the same calling card. How is that even possible? I hate to ask him questions, but I know that the media will only release half the story. Methodically, I get information, pieces at a time. The details are disturbing and eerily similar. Is it possible that someone is watching me, copying me, taunting me? I feel like I'm going to be sick!

I wait until Michael heads off to bed. He has pulled a lot of overtime hours at work, so I know that once he drifts off, there is little to no chance that he will wake back up. Pacing the floor, I feel my patience wearing thin. I'm sweating on every inch of my body. My cheeks are like two cherry tomatoes, and sweat is beading up on my forehead. Michael's briefcase, which is sitting at the foot of the bed, holds all the answers I need. Well, most of them, I hope. Slowly and as quietly as possible, I walk to the edge of the bed, listening to him and carefully analyzing his breathing pattern. I can't chance him waking up and catching me pilfering through his things. Just as I pick up his briefcase, the vibration of his cell phone sitting on the nightstand startles him, and he wakes up. Thankfully, only for a moment. Still, I am frozen in the middle of the room. He rolls back over into a deep sleep, and I am able to sneak out of the room unnoticed.

My heart is beating so fast that I feel faint. It's funny, I don't get this nervous when I'm pulling the trigger. That seems so disturbing to me. I think it's because I feel justified in killing. My sick and twisted spin on vigilante justice. These are not high-functioning people in society; they are bottom feeders, abusing both physically and emotionally many women. Michelle, on the other hand, I feel terrible about killing. I never meant for that to happen. She will never know the sacrifice that I made in hopes of making her life better. I would have done anything for her. Eventually, I will pay restitution for my actions. For now, I have a lot more work that needs to be done. Literally, a hit list a mile long.

My heart rate has finally settled, and I feel somewhat normal again. My time is limited, so I start carefully sifting through all of the papers and documents. They make me seem like a monster, a cold-hearted killer. It makes me sad that they can't see the reason behind the crime. It's obvious they have no leads. John Doe number three, holy fuck! I slam the papers down on the desk and start violently pacing the room and throwing things in anger. They think the same murder weapon was used. What the hell? Would law enforcement fabricate some stupid shit like this just so it seems like they are closing in on the murderer? Do they feel like somehow it would be less traumatic if the community thought there was only one killer? I'm totally losing my shit right now! Clearly, it was not the same murder weapon. I have to launch my own investigation and figure out who the hell John Doe number 3 is. Is this going to be a one-time random occurrence, or is this a real copycat? If this is a copycat, is he or she watching me?

My time is running low; Michael could wake up at any minute. I quickly snap a few pictures on my phone and place them in an encrypted file. I will need these to reference later. I am pleased with the thorough investigation they did with all of my crime scenes. The media always reports that the possible serial killer left the same calling card linking them to the murders but they have never reported what that calling card is. It is clearly photographed and linked to my attacks. Someday, I will use this calling card in my confession. Actually, I spend far more time on my artistic stamp than I do on the actual murder. I did change the stamp slightly for Michelle, and someday I will explain to the rest of the world why.

My dearest Listener,

I'm still deeply saddened by what happened to Michelle. I was only trying to make her life a better place, a safe place where she felt secure, beautiful, appreciated, and valued. This was an epic fail on my part, one that I will pay for the rest of my life. I went through Michael's briefcase and read everything he had in there about the case. I'm so pleased they have acknowledged my calling card. I wasn't sure if they had documented it as of yet because the media was not talking about it. Listener, we have a huge problem. I'm so pissed about it. There was another murder tonight. The police are at a loss and have no leads on either of them, so they are trying to pin the other murder on me. They even said the same murder weapon was used. I think they are saying this to avoid the embarrassment of their failure to catch the other killer. I'm so shocked and disappointed by all of this. Does this shit really happen in real life? Is it possible that our styles are so similar that it would appear to be the same person? This is all making me feel insane.

Thank you for listening, my friend. Your loyalty will never be forgotten. Someday, you will help me tell my story.

Chapter Five

Dusk comes early this time of year. I don't love the cold, but I can't honestly say that I hate it either. It's mild here compared to some parts of the country. I hate the snow and I have no desire to ever live anywhere that produces it.

Traffic is light on my way to the range. It's going to feel so weird walking in there and not seeing Michelle and her beautiful smile. If I'm honest, she actually annoyed me a little, but I know she had a good heart. That's why I did what I did. I did it all to protect her. Jeff was a total dick; he was no good for her. I pull into a space and gather up my things. My usual poker face will hide my emotions, temporarily anyway.

As I enter the building and head down the hall to my stall, I pull the tags off my new gloves and slip them over my fingers. A short, quick flash of a memory sends me into a haze. I can't make this feel weird or it may raise suspicion. One by one, I remove my guns from the case. I load each one of them and prepare my station before sliding my headset over my ears. Round after round I shoot, preparing for the demise of my next victim. I have to be precise and quick, and that's why I come almost every day. With every hour and every bullet I shoot, I perfect my craft. It's a high for me; it's what I live for. Empowering and liberating, it makes me feel safe and allows me to keep others safe.

After several rounds of shooting, I pack up, put on a brave face, and head briskly toward the door. Just steps shy from the door, I hear one of the instructors shout out my name.

"Amy! Sorry I'm out of breath. I literally ran like a cheetah down the hall to catch you. Have you heard about what happened to Michelle? She was found dead last night. We don't have any details yet, but I wanted to make sure you knew."

I lower my head sadly and acknowledge that I have already heard the news.

"I have a few things from her locker, and I know she would have wanted you to have them."

Tears fill my eyes as I respond. "She was a pretty special person to me. I'm going to miss her so much. Thank you for bringing her things to me. You have no idea how much this means."

I drop my head in an attempt to hide my anxiety, and

just as I turn to walk away, she summons me again. "Wait, before you go. I wanted to let you know that we have organized a candlelight vigil tomorrow night to celebrate her life. I hope to see you there."

I turn my head partially around to acknowledge her and nod in response. Walking to the car I totally lose it.

Cassidy and I are having drinks tonight. I think it would be a good time to go through Michelle's things. Right now, I just need some time to think and refocus before I see anyone.

I purposely get home after Michael has left for work. I'm just not ready to see him right now. I'm still so angry at the thought that law enforcement would fabricate a story just to satisfy the palate of societal norms. I hope this is not the case, but I have a sinking suspicion that it is, and I want to pretend that Michael has nothing to do with it. Someday, I want to confront him on all of this, but the timing has to be right.

A quick shower and a change of clothes later, and I'm off to the bar to meet with Cassidy. Despite the chilly temperatures, I'm dressed very Malibu. Perfect highlights in my long, wavy hair glisten as I enter the club with its flashing lights. My dark eyes and dark hair bring a bit of mystery to my game. I walk briskly with purpose toward the bar, making eye contact with no one. I'm really not the social type. I step out just shy of the bar to locate Cassidy before approaching. Glancing side to side I see the shine of brightly colored nails catching the light as Cassidy is waving to get my attention.

"Cassidy!" I bring her in closer to kiss her cheeks.

"Girl, it's so damn good to see you tonight! We have so much to talk about!"

The mood shifts immediately to gray.

"Did you hear about Michelle? I can't believe this has happened. We were just together a few nights ago."

Cassidy takes a long swallow of her cocktail, and we share a quick moment of silence.

"Heather, I'm really struggling with this. Who would want to hurt Michelle? Jeff, I can understand—that guy was a total dick. But who would purposely hurt her? I really need an answer to that!"

I slightly squint my eyes and draw my head back as a blanket of confusion covers my face.

"Wait, Cassidy, you knew Jeff?"

I can tell immediately that she regrets saying it, but isn't sure exactly how to respond.

"I knew of him," she says nervously.

I shake my head gently. How in the hell did Cassidy

know Jeff? What exactly does "know of him" mean? How can you classify someone as a total dick if you barely know them? We're both too emotional to hash out answers, so for now I just need to let it go. I want to drink with my friend and pretend that none of this is really happening!

Sip by sip we share stories about Michelle. I honestly never realized how much the three of us have in common. Cassidy is laughing so hard, she can barely speak. Her dimples are at their widest point on her sweet, innocent face.

"Heather, do you remember the time…?"

Story after story, I sit there, staring at Cassidy in a blind gaze, pretending to be amused, but I am dying inside. Michelle was an amazing person. She was talented, beautiful, and just starting to bloom. Her Kryptonite was dating the wrong men. Narcissistic, abusive men. I never really understood it. Jeff was not even attractive, and he definitely didn't bring much in the way of material things to the table. What exactly did she see in him? Strangely, every time I bring this up to Cassidy, she is indifferent or totally disagrees with me on the subject. This is odd, considering she barely knew him. Tony is not in the least bit arrogant or cocky. He is a kind, generous man who, as far as I know, would do anything for her. That being said, I don't understand why she wouldn't agree with me about

Jeff being an asshole.

My half-empty cocktail glass is dripping with condensation. Still in somewhat of a daze, I take a cocktail napkin and slowly wipe down the glass. Realizing that I need to make myself present in this conversation, I turn the glass up and kill the remaining cocktail, make eye contact with the bartender, and motion for him to bring us both another round. Drowning myself in alcohol seems like a better option right now. As the bartender delivers the two drinks, I notice that he touches Cassidy's hand and whispers, "Make this your last one!" He brushes his pinky against her wrist as he pulls away from her. She turns to me quickly, with panic all over her face, and I have to ask.

"Do you know him?"

She quickly replies, "No, no, I've never met him in my life. I'm not sure what that exchange was about."

After a few minutes of silence, words begin dripping from her lips. Emotionless, she admits to having an affair with him and that she wants it to end, only he isn't exactly willing to do so. "He's threatened that if I stop seeing him, he will ruin my life. I can't let Tony find out about this; he would be crushed."

"What the fuck, Cassidy! You're having an affair?"

I am trying really hard to remain calm, but the asshole behind the bar is not making this an easy task.

THE *Listener*

"Why? Why are you having an affair? Are things not good at home with you and Tony?"

I can tell that she doesn't want to talk about it, so I try not to press the issue.

Cassidy asks, "Can we please just change the subject. It's all I can do right now to deal with Michelle's death. I can't handle this too!"

"Yes, we can shut this down for now, but not forever. I can't allow this man to threaten you." I put my arm around her shoulders, and we move on from the conversation. "I have something I want you to help me do, and I thought we could do this here tonight. They cleaned out Michelle's locker at the gun range and gave her belongings to me."

I set the bag between us on the bar and piece by piece we go through it. Everything we pull out has a story, and we have to tell it in honor of Michelle. It becomes obvious as we look through her things that the people from the gun range were her only or at least closest friends. The last item I pull from the bag is a cell phone. Cassidy quickly grabs it from my hand.

"Hey, can I see that? What the hell is going on, Heather? This is my cell phone. My initials are on the back corner. Oh my God, she knew!"

A confused look crosses my alcohol-flushed face.

"She knew what?"

Cassidy cups her face in her hands and leans into them, crying.

"She knew my secrets," she whispers.

My dearest Listener,

I'm beginning to realize that you are the only one in my life I can trust. The only one who's not keeping secrets from me. Tonight brings so many unanswered questions. The biggest one, why in the hell did Michelle have Cassidy's cell phone in her locker? What secrets of Cassidy's did she hold? Somehow, I have to figure out the answers to these questions. My mission right now is to find out who the hell this bartender is who has shackled my best friend to her mistakes. I don't understand why she's having an affair with this dude, but if he's hurting her by holding her hostage to her indiscretions, then he has to pay. It's been a hell of a day, and I'm ready for it to end. Thank you for allowing me to vent. This eventually will serve penance, as my tongue will be unable to confess…

Chapter Six

Rain crashing against the windowsill and the distant roar of thunder awakens me from a deep, restful sleep. Stormy nights like these wake up the restless souls. Their whispers are haunting, yet the validity of their demise I will never question.

Each and every voice I recognize, yet I feel no remorse. The energy for me is the same. They all deserved to die. Erasing them from society made the world a better place.

"Get out of my head!" I scream as I acknowledge my need for sleep. Realizing their determination is greater, I give in to the pressing desire to take a sleeping pill.

Moments later, I drift off into a deep sleep. Occasionally, my eyes peek open as a flash of lightning dances through the shades. A deeper sleep brings dreams that I will soon forget and nightmares that only come as flashbacks. Tapping into my psyche is Pierre. Literally, the first son of a bitch I had the privilege of killing. His voice is the most haunting, but it carries the most validity to my actions. The evil bastard tortured my best friend. I enjoyed every minute of slaying and

THE *Listener*

delivering his soul into the hands of the devil himself. I was an amateur then, and deep scratches on my face almost ruined my game. For days, I had to hide inside the four walls of my home, panicked and hopeful not to get caught. Another epic law enforcement fail. He was my first, so a serial killer connection was never made. I cleaned his hands well, but I'm sure my DNA remained if tested. I lost my serial killer virginity to him, but it ignited a lust and a constant hunger for revenge blood. My calling card was born that night. His blood was putrid, yet it left a sweet taste on my tongue. I wanted more; it was a high that is hard to explain and few would understand. A necessary evil to make the world a better place. A place where only the good survive.

Over the years my dreams have become more vivid, making it difficult to differentiate them from a vision. Sometimes, the tormented souls speak confessions. Confessions that I know to be true. These confessions have led me to execute differently. I speak my truth to them in a peaceful whisper as I wait for the last signs of life to leave their body. This yields a little peace for my actions. They leave this life with a clear understanding of the "why me" question that plagues them in purgatory. An enjoyable and necessary task, it's a win-win for me.

The loud beeping of my alarm clock startles me out of a deep sleep. My flaccid arm rolls over and hits the snooze for a few extra minutes. As good as it was to lie there, I know I need to get up and leave before Michael gets home from work. I'm not ready to see him and hear the details of his past few nights on patrol. I have to gain a little perspective to avoid being argumentative when he spews the fizzy hypocrisy of there being only being one killer and one murder weapon. Patiently, I will wait to see if this cat strikes again. It could send my desire for the hunt in a different direction. I have a legacy to protect, and this is my turf. These lines I will not allow to be crossed.

Half-awake I crawl out of bed and into a hot shower. Steam from the moist heat summons a blanket of fog on the glass door and the mirrors behind it. I lather up with a lavender-scented body wash and slowly massage every inch of my body. Liberating, once you discover all the magnificence of satisfying yourself. A perfect way to start the day.

I slip into a dress suit and head out the door. The local coffee shop will be my savior in a few short minutes. Today, I embark on a new journey. A journey to seduce a dance of death with a bartender who will satisfy my lust and seal his fate.

My dearest Listener,

    I can't get over the arrogance of this guy we met at the bar. Oddly, I found him erotic and a bit mysterious. I may have to explore him on a deeper level before taking him from this life. I will wait a few weekends to hopefully erase the meeting of me and my association with Cassidy from his mind. This will not be an easy task, as I consider myself unforgettable. I keep having visions of us having sex. This morning in the shower, I moaned with pleasure imagining his tongue dancing and massaging me into pure ecstasy. This one is going to be fun to play with.

    I want to thank you for your loyalty to me… Thank you for listening.

Chapter Seven

My favorite part about walking into a coffee shop is the overwhelming smell of brewing espresso and the mindless chatter of eager patrons patiently waiting for their morning fix. Admittedly, I'm plagued with the malignancy of a caffeine addiction. It's intoxicating really.

Slowly, I make my way through the line, grab my coffee, and head off to work. Ready to face the world, but, oh my freaking God, not ready at all to face… Holy shit! It's him! It's the bartender from the bar. I quickly make eye contact and say hello. Realizing that I need a quick distraction, I drop my coffee on the ground in front of him.

"Oh my goodness, I'm so terribly sorry!"

He quickly reaches down and grabs the cup, insisting that there is no harm done. I extend a warm hand out to him.

"Hello, I'm Heather, and you are?"

Not at all surprised by my gesture, he confidently responds with a quick, brisk handshake.

"Blaze. It's my pleasure to make your acquaintance this morning. Can I buy you another coffee?"

THE *Listener*

Assuming that I won't decline his generous offer, he motions, with a wave of his hand, both of us back into the coffee shop. Once inside, we order and find a quiet little table in the corner for our impromptu rendezvous. He's a smooth talker and a seasoned operator. Literally dripping with cockiness. I'm soaking it all up. This one will be easy to attract into my dark web of fate.

"Blaze, my curiosity overcomes my ability to assume silence and be nonjudgmental. I have to ask, is this a nickname or did your mother have nothing left in her repertoire of ideas to give?"

A name like Blaze is undeniably a birthright or a cruel albatross that deviates from traditional norms. Either way, I have to know. He takes a sip of his coffee and with a serious glare he responds,

"Blaze is my birth name. I'm not completely sure where it came from, yet, here it is. It's definitely a topic of conversation with just about everyone I meet. I like it and I really like you. I have to head to work, but is there any chance that I could be graced with your beautiful smile again?"

As he stands up and starts to tidy up his area, I see a flash of what looks like a wedding ring. I suspect that he has been making a conscious effort to hide it from me all morning. I purse my lips out and seductively make eye contact.

"I would love to see you again. Let's just cut out all of the nonsensical dancing, pretending we're not here for the same reason. This entire morning has been about lust. We're both married. Here's my digits; send me a text of a place and time that suits you. I'm soaking wet with desire, so make it soon!"

I wink at him, hand over my number, and walk away. I can literally see his desire for me growing as I "blaze" my path to the door.

My dearest Listener,

I met and spent an hour of mindless chatter this morning with my next victim. The sexual tension was explosive as we exchanged pleasantries. Depending on his actions going forward, I may have to keep this one around a bit. His narcissism was palpable. I love that in a man. Well, allow me to clear that statement up a bit. I don't love a narcissistic man; I love to play with them. I play with their mind and ease my way into their heart. This makes for an easy target. I allow him to think he's saving me, but all the while he's literally killing himself. For some reason I'm drawn to this type of man sexually and a little bit intellectually. It's intriguing how the mind works. If I hate narcissism so much, why do I love being with narcissists, especially in bed? Blaze checks all of the boxes for me. He's going to be delicious.

Here is the dark side to all of this. While we are in bed, I give him the illusion of control. I let him call the shots and manhandle me in every way possible. I like it rough. I want and crave total disrespect. Spit on me, choke me…

these are my desires. All the while, all I can think about is how I'm going to kill him and how his blood is going to taste dripping from my lips. All of these things are dancing in my head as I moan with satisfaction. It's a little sick and demented, but I crave it. I have homed in on the smell of fear. It's a wild instinct but I have it.

There's something evil that lives inside of me. From the outside, I'm this perfect person. An accomplished woman in a perfect marriage and life. I'm happy, or at least I think I am. On the inside, I'm a monster.

Chapter Eight

Selling the sunset could not end fast enough today. Expectations have been exhausted, and my primal instincts are creeping in. I'm starving. Michael and I are meeting for dinner, and I'm fully prepared for an unsolicited dump of inaccurate information about a triple homicide conveniently stamped as being related. Over the years I've mastered the art of pretending to buy into frivolous bullshit. Tonight, it will be no different.

Anxiously, I close up the Malibu estate and head to Nobu to meet Michael. Upon arrival, I scan the place to see if I know anyone. I'm not an antisocial person, but sometimes I just prefer to be alone. Well, as alone as I can be having dinner with my husband. While scanning the room, I quickly locked eyes with Mike. After all of these years, it still excites me to see him. Joyfully, I bounce over to him and kiss him on the cheek. He seems indifferent and clearly bothered by something.

"Hey, baby, it's good to see you. Are you okay?" I ask in a concerned voice.

He pauses for a moment and appears to be thinking before he answers.

"I'm okay, I guess. As okay as I can be right now. Things at work are really stressing me out. This serial killer is making a fool out of our department. Last night, a triple homicide!" Michael leans in and whispers, "He killed three people! Three, with the same murder weapon, and not a single trace of DNA was left behind. We are at a total loss!"

Sweat is beading up on his forehead, and his anxiety is palpable.

"Michael, how can you be so sure the same person killed all three of those people? How is that even possible?"

Anxiously, I await his answer, trying desperately not to show a physical response.

"We know because he leaves his mark, a calling card of his own design making sure that he gets credit for his kill. It's a heart traced with the blood of the victim. Every heart is designed almost exactly the same."

"All three of them have the same calling card?" I respond quickly without thinking it through.

"Exactly!" Michael replies in anger. "Heather, I have to ask you a question, and I need you to tell me the truth. Did you go through my briefcase? Wait, let me rephrase my question. Why did you go through my briefcase? Don't lie. I already know that you did! I just need to know why."

I don't know how to respond. Either way, this is going to be an uncomfortable confrontation to have in a restaurant. Still waiting on our food, Michael can sense my hesitation. He slams his hand harshly on the table and whispers in a low but angry voice, "Let's go!"

I don't question him. I just grab my purse and head to the door. The heaviness of the glares are piercing as patrons become curiously invested in our tabletop drama.

Driving separately gives me the opportunity to cultivate a believable story. Obviously, Michael knows that I was in his briefcase, so clearly there is no reason to deny it. I need to quickly come up with a believable scenario.

My eyes are glassy and cheeks a rosy red as my anxiety heightens to an insane level. The closer I get to the house, the more palpable my guilt becomes. I can taste the bitterness of my own fury. He makes it home before me, and the garage door is already open. I pull in, hit the lights, and head into the house. Knowing damn well that my performance has to be top-notch, I go straight to the bar for some liquid courage. He walks in casually behind me and seemingly with zero panic attached. The silence as he enters the room is deafening, and I have to break the ice.

"Michael, I'm sorry I went through your things. It has nothing to do with you or us. This case is making me crazy, and I have so many questions. I need answers! Cassidy and I are out there all day every day showing houses, and I know damn well that the media is not telling us the truth! Curiosity set in, my moral compass failed me, and I violated your privacy. For that, I'm incredibly sorry."

He just stands there, but not without emotion. I can see his desire for me hardening by the moment. My anger turns him on and awakens his lustful, immature, boyish libido. It always has and of course knowing this, I use sexually driven anger to get my way. This has worked well for me in the past. He wants to throw me against the wall and punish me with his throbbing cock. His predictability has worked well for me over the years.

"Michael, are you going to respond?"

He slightly nods and takes a few sips of bourbon. He pulls me closer to him and seductively unbuttons my blouse. I'm soaked with desire. I reach down to unbutton his jeans and everything changes. He gently pushes my hands away and places his fingers on my lips, rolls them back and forth, and says, "Baby, you deserve a daytime Emmy for that theatrical production!"

He refills his bourbon glass, and with a great deal of cockiness, he walks away.

My dearest Listener,

One of two things is happening here. I have Michael totally fooled or he's on to me. This could go either way. He absolutely cannot live without me, and because of that, he may be willing to overlook and possibly help cover up some things. I wouldn't want to willingly say that he put me in my place, but he put me in my place. I'm not going to push the issue and question it. My mission right now is Blaze. He's the object of my desire. Good night, my friend.

Chapter Nine

A daytime Emmy? If he only knew the extent of sarcasm that he just spewed. The mystery to me would be a police department, quite literally dripping with cockiness, yet they have no leads on a crime committed by an amateur assassin. It's likely I will be upgraded to a seasoned serial killer by the time they sniff out my trail. Sad considering the sloppiness of my previous murders, especially Pierre. There was an incredible amount of rage when I slayed his narcissistic ass. I didn't even play with him first. Needless to say, it wasn't very thought out!

Pierre had been dating my sister for a couple of years, and she was completely enamored with him. I could never put my finger on her reasons as to why. Personally, nothing about the sorry bastard appealed to me. Just like me, she was drawn to the cockiness and picturesque physique of the classic gym rat. I get it—it's a negative burn to our Italian lineage. We have a lustful eye and a weakness for the designer man made by the roid. They must be good in bed, right? Tastefully delicious to the eye and pure

THE *Listener*

satisfaction elsewhere. Sorry to disappoint, but this is a total fallacy, the epitome of false advertisement. The truth is, they're yummy to look at but a sheer disappointment between the sheets. Yet somehow, shallow desire overrides common sense. Literally, every single time!

Killing Pierre wasn't well planned, and the execution was extremely sloppy. Stereotypical, amateur mistakes that give the passionate vigilante serial killer a bad name. Honestly, it should have landed me in prison. Yet somehow I got away with it. I got away with murder. Powered by a surge of angry emotions, I took a bat to the back of his head, splattering blood all over the place, and walked away, leaving no trace of DNA. I was fearful for months, yet the pure satisfaction of taking the life of a man who tormented my sister for so many years lit a fire in me like no other. The hunt was now in my blood, and my constant desire to taste it grew to epic proportions. I craved the smell of fear and the metallic taste of sweet revenge.

※

Just as I am settling in for the evening, the jingle of my phone startles me. I grab it and quickly look at the screen. It is Blaze! A spark of excitement lights my next fire. I take a sip of wine and eagerly hit the accept call button.

"Hello, Blaze!" I answer in a sultry, come-hither voice.

"Heather, it's so good to hear your voice. I hope it's not too late to call. I've been thinking about you all day."

While it turns me on that I was in his thoughts all day, I know damn well that Cassidy was in his bed all afternoon. Deep inside his perpetually boyish mind I'm sure were thoughts of both of us! Classic! I hold back my sharp tongue in an effort to preserve the moment. He is hot and I desire him. His cockiness is a huge turn-on, and I always play with my food before eating it.

"Blaze, that's so hot that you've been thinking about me. Care to share your thoughts? I have a better idea; let's plan to get together, and you can act them out. We both know where this is going. There's no reason to waste copious amounts of time on meaningless conversation."

He hesitates in his response but takes me up on my offer. I sweeten the deal.

"Actually, Blaze, Michael is working tonight. We had an argument right before he left for work, and I have an insane amount of rage and sexual energy to release. Do you want to come over and help me out with that?"

Quick to respond and without hesitation, he is on his way over. I have this innate superpower in that I know when a man is going to rock my world in bed. There's no doubt that Blaze is going to do it for me. I will use him a few times, gain his trust, and then release him to the other world.

THE *Listener*

Just before his arrival I open the garage door to allow him to park inside and hopefully go unnoticed. While on patrol, Michael frequently drives by the house. One would think this would make me nervous, but it's quite the opposite. I get aroused by it; it's a high for me. It's the Russian roulette of raw, raunchy sex.

We bring our glasses together and tap to a deadly dance of fate. A dance that I have become quite familiar with, deliciously dark and designed by me. Blaze will launch me into uncharted territory, only I don't know it yet.

My dearest Listener,

My confessions tonight will blow your mind. I'm not really sure if I'm ready to admit them, even to you. But your loyalty to me has proven worthy, so here goes.

My signature game of "lust is trust" backfired tonight, and I'm finding myself in uncharted territory. There's something very different about him. His elusive yet strong sense of confidence pulled me in, and our explosive chemistry together is pleading with me to stay. While I would like to play with him for a while, I have this strong gut feeling that he's going to need to go quickly. I know he is a bad person, and the feelings I've developed for him after one night of passion aren't real. He's a classic narcissist and on top of his game. That's what I thought anyway. Maybe he's not. Now I'm thinking his actions toward Cassidy that night came from a place of protection and not control, but where do I go from here? My exploration of him must be short-lived as my desires for him could blur the mission. I have to remain focused. For now my need for sleep is overwhelming me, so I must go. Sweet dreams to you, my dearest friend, my listener.

Chapter Ten

Nightfall… It awakens my troubled soul, further confirming the viability of evil flowing freely in the depths of my mind. Yet, I feel no remorse. My actions are validated in an effort to make the world a better place. No good deed goes unpunished, and the evil that surrounds me spares no expense tormenting my soul night after night as I close my eyes to sleep. My visions are getting stronger and almost nightly. Frozen in fear, I lie in my bed and just listen, allowing every victim to have a voice, a unique story to tell. My body stiffens and my eyes roll back into my head, leading to uncontrollable paralysis. The sound of distant thunder is controlling my mind. He presents himself to me wearing a black hooded sweatshirt and a facial covering similar to that of a balaclava. Demanding that I not speak, he forcibly places two fingers over my lips and pushes my shoulders against the bed.

"Does Cassidy know what you've done? Does she? She was everything to me. Michelle knew! She knew everything and I planned to get rid of her, and everything she knew would go away. Why couldn't you just wait? Now, Cassidy will never know how much I loved her! I was willing to kill for her, but so were you. You evil bitch, you will pay for this. You will pay!"

In my dream he left as quickly as he came.

Foam is dripping from my mouth, and the heat from my body soaks the sheets in sweat.

"Jeff! Jeff! Jeff!"

I scream his name over and over. It is deafening. Cassidy was having an affair with Jeff, and Michelle must have found out about it. That could be why she had her phone. Cassidy must have left it at Jeff's, and Michelle inadvertently retrieved it and all of the secrets it held. I want so badly to confront Cassidy about all of this, but unfortunately, that's not going to be an option.

Exhausted, I crawl out of bed and head to the shower. Sarcastically, I shout out to Jeff, thanking him for clearing a whole lot of shit up. I'm tired but I have to stay on my game. Cassidy and I are working together, and after work we have dinner plans with the guys.

Waiting for the shower to heat up, I disrobe and face the mirror to brush my teeth. My shoulder is red, and there are scratches with spots of blood trailing down my arm. That bastard. I'm glad I killed his sorry ass. I don't care how much he claims he loved Cassidy; he was an

THE *Listener*

asshole to Michelle and I knew it. No one deserves to be treated the way he treated her and countless others I'm sure! I have no regrets, and if I had the chance to do it all over again, I would.

While in the shower I put very little thought into my dreams. Putting everything out of my mind, I quickly wash my hair, get dressed, and start my day. Despite my lack of sleep, I feel quite amazing.

Feeling sexy and on my game, I turn, face the mirror, and take a full body selfie and send it to Blaze. I can't get him off my mind, and I'm determined to remain fresh in his. I press the send button, grab my purse, and head out the door. Cassidy and I are showing a house today in Malibu. Malibu pretty much sells itself, as it is laden with money and power. The colossal epitome of the financial ecosystem that is Southern California. Everyone has a lawyer, a private doctor, and a detail team that closely resembles the lineup on Magic Mike. Call me silly, but having that much money is senseless, if not torture. When you have that much, what is there left to look forward to?

Steps from the ocean, this luxurious pad is quite literally made of glass. Oversized sliding doors open up, allowing a monstrous sea breeze to blow throughout the house. The house is horseshoe shaped and wraps itself around the most unique infinity pool I've ever seen. Unlike any other, it is made entirely of decorative Italian handmade tile. I've honestly never seen anything like it in my life. As the day gives way to evening, lights illuminate the vibrant colors throughout the pool. Truly, a decadent treat for the seasoned eye.

As the work day comes to a close, I find myself deep in thought about Blaze. I can't get him off my mind. This is uncharted territory for me as I have never had a desire to continue a relationship with one of my victims. It's always been "lust to trust" only. He is different somehow, yet I can't put my finger on it. I'm having weird jealousy issues about him and Cassidy. I can't help but wonder if they're still seeing each other.

"Cassidy!" I yell with a spark of excitement. "It's time to go meet our guys at Nobu! I'm starving, how about you?"

Without hesitation she responds, "I'm famished and I could use a cocktail!"

"Hell yes!" I exclaim. "Brace yourself, Cassidy. I'm sure the topic of conversation tonight will be that bloody serial killer. I don't know how much Tony has told you, but they suspect the three murders that took place the other night were the work of the same person. I have a really hard time believing it, but that's what they are reporting. Has Tony discussed any of this with you?"

Cassidy pauses. "Actually, he did. He said the killer used the same calling card at both scenes. Apparently, he wanted to make a clear statement of credit. I'm just sick of all of this. I haven't been able to properly mourn Jeff's and Michelle's deaths."

A troubled and curious look fills my peaked face.

"There it is again, Cassidy! Twice now you've made mention of Jeff. How well did you know him?"

Heaviness fills the air around us as obvious discomfort terminates our conversation. Wanting to make this as comfortable as possible, I choose to let it go and not press her for information. Dinner tonight is going to be tumultuous enough without me making things worse.

We enter the restaurant, and the guys are already seated and drinks have been ordered. I sigh with relief, as alcohol will tame the situation pretty quickly. This will be the first time seeing Michael since our argument. Sexual tension is high, but I dare not initiate anything tonight. Not after the cruel way he shot me down. Not that I didn't deserve it, but he certainly didn't know that. For now, I will feed into his egotistical, narcissistic trip and give the illusion that he is in control.

Despite my expectations of a miserable night, it actually unfolds quite nicely. Tony and Michael purposely keep work out of our evening together. It is like old times.

It escapes my understanding how Cassidy and I have the perfect life, yet we still feel the need for extramarital affairs. For me, it's just to gain trust, an essential part of the hunt. For Cassidy, it seems to be on a deeper level. A more dangerous level. She isn't happy at home, and if she is, she clearly wants more. I've spent a lot of time lately thinking about what it means to be happy. Oftentimes, I think we can mistake unhappiness for settling into a routine. The newness and excitement wear off, leaving us to seek out something with a little more mystery. I have this gravitational pull toward cockiness. It's an addiction really. When I was younger, I thought it was the confidence that I was drawn to. While this may hold some level of truth, on a deeper level it's the feeling of dominance and control. I want to be dominated.

Chapter Eleven

A surge of childlike excitement sends shock waves through my body as the pulse of my alarm clock awakens me. Michael is working a double today, so I took the day off to be with Blaze. While I know I have exceeded my "lust to trust" rules with him, I'm just not ready to release him back into the wild.

Close to his arrival time, I open up a bottle of wine and slip into some sexy lingerie. I want to be one glass ahead of him at all times. I do this in an effort to forget the deceptively dark meaning driving our relationship.

A slight creaking sound of the door startles me as he softly pushes it open and slowly walks toward me. No words are spoken between us, and the tension is thick as thieves. I set down my wineglass and reach out for him, summoning him to me. I pull his lips into mine and passionately kiss him. Our tongues dance together, and I can feel his desire for me as I place one hand in his jeans and stroke him softly. Sex with Blaze is hot and unbridled. A meaningless journey to places I've never been before. I connect with him on a much different level. I think that our late night conversations are to blame. We spend copious amounts of time talking to each other. Actually, we talk far more than we have sex, and this may be where things go terribly wrong. I start to feel him as a person, someone I could love.

To end our time together, we go into the city for an early dinner. Los Angeles is really just a big small town. Huge and uncomfortable if you aren't from here, but quite comfortable if you are. That's one of the many things I love about living here; it's life by design. It can be whatever you want it to be.

We settle comfortably into an intimate corner of one of my favorite Italian bistros. The salivating aroma of the freshly baked bread, blended with an Italian spice I don't quite recognize, fills the air around us. As tantalizing as the aroma is, I really just want a bottle of their best wine to accompany the conversation with Blaze. His cheeks are flushed and eyes are glazed, making his nervousness about being there with me a bit more obvious. Trying to focus on our conversation is difficult as my mind keeps drifting off to a better place. This guy is incredibly gorgeous. The kind of gorgeous I never imagined happening for me, although I envied it in other people. We pause our chat for a brief moment as the waiter returns with another bottle of wine. We gaze deliciously into one another's eyes as he opens and pours us both a fresh glass.

"Heather, I have something I want to tell you; it's really been bothering me."

I hesitate for a moment. The sincerity in his voice is troubling.

"Okay, you sound so serious. I hope it's nothing bad."

He holds eye contact with me and then he places both hands around the top of his head. He looks down and takes a deep breath. "I guess it depends on your definition of bad. My feelings for you, Heather, are far beyond sexual. The sex is amazing, but there's so much more. At the risk of hurting you, I have to come clean about something. Your friend Cassidy and I have been having an affair for a couple of years. When you were together in the bar that night, it was so hard for me to pretend not to know her and not to want to get to know you. When I saw you a few days later coming out of the coffee shop, I almost lost my mind. I have enjoyed every minute with you, and I don't want this to end, but I think I need to end things with Cassidy."

I focus on my wineglass. I just can't make eye contact with him right now. How can I pretend not to know? I could totally see this coming, and truthfully, the feeling is mutual.

"You've been seeing each other for a year? She's my best friend. How could I not know this? Tell me about your relationship. A year is a long time. Are you in love with her?"

I'm still staring down at my glass and not wanting to look up. He gently places his hand on my chin and pushes it up. In a soft voice he says, "Look at me, Heather. Cassidy and I have been together for a while, but honestly, I have never felt this way about her. I have never felt this way about anyone. I have to know if you feel the same. Do you have feelings for me, or is this just sexual for you?"

The truth is, I do have feelings for Blaze, but this is not how it's supposed to work. I messed up. If he breaks up with Cassidy, do I terminate the plan? He made the hit list because I felt a narcissistic vibe when he was interacting with her that night at the bar. Maybe I read him all wrong. I'm so confused right now, and I need to sort this all out of my head before I present an answer to him. I have to find a gentle way to put him on hold.

"Blaze, I'm having trouble processing all of this. This is not the conversation I expected to be having with you right now, or ever. I have a question for you before I answer. How will this affect your relationship with Cassidy going forward? Does my answer dictate whether or not you break up with her? I'm not sure how I feel about any of this. She's my best friend and my partner at the real estate office."

With no hesitation he says, "No, your answer does not affect how I handle my relationship with her. I would feel terrible if I continued seeing her now that I realize I'm not truly in love with her. That would be wrong on so many levels, and I'm not that guy. It honestly took meeting you to realize that my feelings for her aren't real. I can't just keep her around for sex. That's not the kind of man I am. So, to answer your question, I'm going to break it off with her either way. I just didn't want you to find out from anyone else but me. I respect your decision and I respect your decision not to answer right now. I just needed you to know. I'm sorry about all of this. I truly am."

Holy shit! Processing all of this is going to be a challenge. Fact and problem number one would be that I'm now questioning the charges I made against him. He seems genuine and the flavor he presented tonight has no taste of narcissism. How could I have misjudged him this much? I judged him based on his whispers that night at the bar.

"Give me some time to figure all of this out. Blaze, I have feelings for you, I admit that, but I'm also married. The hardest thing is going to be Cassidy. How is she going to feel about this? Michael is going to be home soon, so I have to go. Let's finish this glass and call it a night."

In complete silence we sit. I'm so lost right now. I just need this night to end!

My dearest Listener,

I can't totally deny that I didn't see this coming. My confusion about Blaze deepened tonight when he shared his feelings for me. After spending time with him, it's become painfully obvious that I may have misjudged him. The lines of our relationship have been blurred, and I'm really struggling. If I'm being honest, Listener, I'm in love with him, and I don't want to let go, even if it means losing Cassidy or even Michael. I can't believe I'm admitting this, even to you. I do question my feelings. Am I sure that I misjudged him for being a narcissist, or is he really that good? Is it possible that I'm foolishly fooled, dickmatized, or naive? I have to refocus and pick a lane. I judged him on one incident, and maybe that wasn't enough. I almost feel like I have to take into consideration that Cassidy is having multiple affairs. There was Jeff, who was definitely an asshole, and then there's Blaze. At some point I have to question Cassidy's judgment. I think in some weird, demented way, I'm using this as an excuse to exit our friendship with very little guilt.

For the most part Michael and I have a functional relationship at best. We're very close, but we do have our vices and underlying sins. Honestly, it would not take much for me to walk away from him. If anyone in my life could get me to do that, it would be Blaze. I have to put this all into perspective and put a lot more thought into it.

Thank you for listening. I'm exhausted and my evening is not near being over, but it helps to talk. You're all I have, I trust you.

Chapter Twelve

Dense fog and total darkness make for a miserable journey home. As challenging as it is, it allows me the necessary time alone that I need to sort this all out in my head…and my heart. Surprisingly, I'm not struggling with this decision as much as I should be. I'm strong and evolved enough to admit when I'm wrong, and I know in my heart that I'm wrong.

Fumbling all over the passenger seat, I search for my cell phone, which I carelessly tossed over when I entered the car. The soft humming sound of a vibration alerts me of a message. It is Blaze. Excitement and utter confusion send the same shock waves to my brain, signaling immediate procrastination. Inside the garage I sit shrouded in confusion and guilt. I can feel the heat rising in my cheeks, and my eyes are starting to burn and tear up. As I hold my phone cupped between my hands, tears start to fall and I just let them. I need to get this all out. I beg the question, am I crying for me or is this a feeble yet honest attempt to recalibrate my moral compass? I have created a cesspool of dark decisions, and my integrity literally hangs in the balance. How did I get here, backed into this corner that I will have to silently fight my way out of?

In my hands the vibration of my phone sends my anxiety to a whole new level. Now Cassidy is calling. It's very unusual for her to be calling this late at night, so I feel that I have no other choice but to answer. With very little time to pull myself together, I hit the accept call button.

"Hello."

Cassidy's voice is broken and I can tell she isn't okay. I wait patiently for her to speak. I know she will when she is ready.

"Heather, I really need to talk to you. It's important. Can you get away and meet me somewhere?"

My heart is beating out of my chest, and my anxiety level is at a solid ten. I'm in no place tonight to be dealing with anyone else's self-destructive decisions. Realizing that I have no other choice, I agree to meet with her. Michael and Tony are working overnight tonight, so I invite her over.

Quickly, I run inside the house and take a quick shower in hopes of pulling my shit together before her arrival. A valiant effort and two glasses of wine later, Cassidy arrives at the door. I straighten my top and reach out to open the door. We hug and exchange pleasantries before driving into the conversation that very literally makes me sick. Cassidy came to spill the tea on her relationship with Blaze.

Swimming in a sea of hypocritical déjà vu, I attempt to listen and pretend to be in a state of shock. Could this night honestly get any worse? I need someone to get us all out of this soap opera melodrama and kill one of us. I don't even care which one, but it needs to happen before my best friend finds out the truth.

"Heather, I have to vent for a bit. My heart is heavy and I need someone to talk to. Someone who will understand and not judge me. You have always been my ride or die, and I know that I can trust you!"

Shrouded in guilt, I summon her to continue.

"Remember that night at the bar where you and I went to talk about Michelle? That night was a little stressful for me. I was struggling dealing with losing Michelle, but there was so much more. Do you remember the bartender?"

I hesitate to give the illusion that I am trying to remember.

"I do remember him. He was hot, bald, and had an incredible body. He was tattooed and had blue eyes. Am I on the right track?"

"Yes, I knew you would remember him. He's definitely our type. Well, I've been having an affair with him for over two years."

Pausing for the moment, I pull myself together before spewing my hypocritical swill of deception.

"What the hell, Cassidy? You're having an affair? How have you been able to hide this from Tony for so long? Whoa, that guy is a freaking beast! Honestly, I can totally see the attraction you have for him. Tell me this, if this has been going on for more than two years, why are you telling me this tonight, and why do you seem so upset?"

"Heather, I think he may be seeing someone else. If not, he is definitely losing interest, and it's killing me inside. We had plans tonight, and he canceled at the last minute. He never does that. He's just not the same when he's with me anymore. I think he's even losing interest in sex. When we're together, it doesn't feel like he's there, if you know what I mean. Emotionally, he's totally absent. I know you're not going to agree or support me in any of this, but if you could offer advice as a friend, I would really appreciate it. I could use a friend right now."

I take a moment to breathe and process before responding.

"Cassidy, I don't know what to say. You know I love you, and I will support any decision you make. I'm just a little shell shocked right now. Putting our friendship with you and Tony as a couple aside, I will offer my advice. I think you may be overreacting and prematurely jumping to conclusions. You have been together for two years; do you think he may be just getting comfortable rather than losing interest? I think that is very common in a relationship. Have you talked about leaving Tony and being with him full time?"

"It's funny that you asked that, Heather. I tried to bring it up a few days ago, and he just shut me down."

As the evening progresses, the conversation falls deeper and deeper into the vast trenches of everything that accompanies the sin of infidelity. Cassidy is a total basket case right now, and I cannot begin to imagine the dark path this will take if she finds out the truth. I have to protect her; she is my best friend. My ride or die.

"Cassidy, I have to wonder, how does your relationship with Tony play into all of this? Are you guys having problems? Two years seems like a really long time to hide an affair. What I'm trying to ask is, are you happy? I'm with you every day. Have I overlooked your unhappiness?"

Sarcastically Cassidy brings her wineglass to her lips and rolls her eyes side to side.

"Define happy."

Realizing that this night will not soon end, I open up another bottle of wine. The third of the night, lowering my anxiety level one sip at a time. My feeble attempt to counsel Cassidy is riddled with hypocrisy.

"Cassidy, I have to ask, if this has been going on for this long, then why are you so upset tonight? Are you in love with him? I know it's hard to suspect that he may be seeing someone else, but in the big scheme of things—and when I say scheme, I'm referring to your relationship with Tony—how much does it really matter? Don't you love him too? I mean, I totally get it. Michael and Tony are broken from the same mold. They can be complicated, but so can we. What we have is safe and comfortable. Are you willing to risk losing all of that?"

Pausing only for a brief moment, Cassidy decides to unleash years of built-up, suppressed anxiety and animosity.

"Heather, you think you know Tony, but you don't. You see only the light in him. Let me show you his darkness. He has cheated on me for years. Literally, one affair after another. He barely comes up for air before he beds the next one. He does very little to try to hide it. I know that Michael knows, and I'm surprised he hasn't told you, unless he has secrets himself. Every woman he dicks down is a trophy for him. He is shallow and passionless when it comes to me. Having sex is just a routine. I am his gift of innocence, and I really just want to be his dirty little whore. Why can't I be both? I was playing his own game, getting back at him for years of infidelity when I fell in love with Blaze. Here is another bomb I need to drop tonight.

THE *Listener*

He is not my first affair. There have been countless others. Unfortunately, my revenge has taken a very dark turn. I'm in love with another man, and it's torture because I know deep down that I cannot have him."

The silence in the room is deafening and heavy.

"Heather, say something, please!"

"I'm without words. I don't know what to say. This is a lot for me to process. Why have you kept this all bottled up all these years? I'm your best friend, yet you felt like you couldn't share any of this with me. This is abuse and you of all people don't deserve this. I'm so angry right now! I should really calm down before I say something that I can't take back. You can't stay in this marriage; it will destroy every part of you. It will eat away at your self-worth, and that, my friend, is hard to come back from."

With tears in her eyes Cassidy screams, "Then be my ride or die—help me get out of this!"

In a low, firm voice I reply, "I'm your ride or die."

My Dearest Listener,

What a night! I don't even know where to begin. My relationship with Blaze just reached an epic level of complication. Twenty hours ago I thought my hardest decision was dealing with Blaze. At that moment the task felt insanely difficult. After spending the evening with Cassidy, that task feels almost obsolete. I mean, what exactly did she mean by "be my ride or die"? Are we eliminating Tony or Blaze? What the heck is going on, and how the hell are we going to deal with this? I can't wrap my head around any of this! Does she want to remove Blaze to make her life less complicated, or does she want to get rid of Tony as some form of marital revenge? I have no choice but to help her. She is my best friend, and I have a moral obligation to see this through. My question to you would be this. Do I handle this shit and act alone, or do we truly ride or die?

I've got some big decisions to make here. I'm learning for the first time tonight that Tony is abusive and

THE *Listener*

apparently having multiple affairs. I definitely didn't see this coming! Tony seems like a kind and gentle man. I've always said, you never really know somebody. Everyone has a dark side.

Chapter Thirteen

I'm craving the taste of blood so badly that it's quite literally all I can think about. Day after day my need for another victim overrides my moral desire to kill for the right reason. Sitting in a dark corner of an LA nightclub, I scope out my next fix. Disregarding every signal and questioning the efficacy of my moral compass, I smooth-talk my way into the arms of the perfect, imperfect gentleman. He is a tall chap with dark skin and the most incredible eyes I've ever seen. They are dark with a distinguished squint-like slant when he smiles. He is very sexy. His hair is black and a bit longer than I prefer on a man, but he carries it well. His level of confidence is off the charts, as the obvious obsession with steroids and injectable testosterone is not amiss. This is classic! He's going to be easy. His name is Mario; that's going to be delicious rolling off my tongue tonight. I have a thing for names. The name has to be as attractive as the person. I could never be with a Dick or a Bob, and I hate the name Peter. It's weird, I know, but it's the magic that is me. In this case I guess it really doesn't matter. My goal is to end and not start a life tonight.

The eye contact and sexual energy increase with the continuous flow of drinks. Excitement sends chills up and down my spine as a once innocent conversation turns into pure lust. I'm in the middle of telling him a story, and he places his hand softly against my neck and brings it to him and kisses me. Our tongues dance together as I imagine his tongue dancing between my legs. Unbridled primal desire leaves my panties hot and wet. Ready for him to make his move, I reach down to feel his desire for me. He is hard and this is making my contractions stronger. I'm incredibly aroused, and my nipples are getting hard and uncomfortable. I'm horny as fuck and I want him now. I lean in to him and whisper in his ear.

"Is there somewhere we can go?"

Without hesitation he responds, "Let's go to my place. I live in the Hills."

Assuming that he isn't married, I quickly accept his request. The Hills is a swanky district in Beverly Hills. He must have money, and with money comes status. If I go to his house, my DNA will be all over the place. Right now I'm too horny to care, and my decision-making skills are lacking. This is not good.

"Mario, we just met and I hate to break the vibe, but can we go to a secluded area and do this in the wild?"

With a shocked look on his face he responds, "In the wild, like outside?"

Judging by his response I can only assume that he has never experienced any level of intimacy in the wild. I have to be creative in my response.

"Mario, I have the perfect idea. Let's go!"

We run into a side alley street. I stop in the darkness and pull his face to mine. With barely enough light to see each other's face, I reach down, grab the bottom of my shirt, and pull it off. He cups my breasts in his hands and seductively starts licking my neck. His whispers are almost chant-like, and it's sending a surge of hormonal chills up and down my spine. My hands are inside his pants, stroking him, and he forcibly spins me around and pushes me against the wall. With one hand on my neck and the other on the wall, he pushes and strokes until I'm screaming with pleasure. His timing choking me is impeccable, and the release increases the intensity of my orgasm tenfold. This experience is so amazing that I'm actually having second thoughts about killing him.

Without a word exchanged between us, he zips up his pants and proceeds to leave the alley without me. I certainly pegged this narcissistic asshole accurately! In frustration I call out to him.

"Hey, Mario, are you just going to leave me here alone?"

He lifts up his hand and fires off a slight wave and keeps on walking. I know exactly where he is parked, so I take a different route to his car so that he can see me approach him. I want him to see me! I didn't have time to torture him tonight. I gave him the best sex of his life as a send-off, and that is going to have to be gift enough. With very little space left between us, I call out his name, bring up my .45, and send him to meet his maker.

Working quickly, I put on one glove, taste the fear in his blood, and leave my calling card on the pavement beside him. My quickest and honestly my most liberating kill yet!

I take off my shoes, and with my gloves still on, I walk calmly over to my car. It could be hours before his body is found. I work smarter when I'm not in a hurry. Tonight, my primal desire for unbridled, spontaneous sex and the taste of blood led me to uncharted territory. Never have I sought out to kill without weeks of planning and premeditating every single detail. It was primal and incredibly delicious. I loved every minute of it.

Overwhelmed with the satisfaction of outsmarting a classic narcissist, I drive home feeling very little to absolutely no remorse. It's quite the opposite actually. I feel empowered and liberated. I have no fear of getting caught. This transaction was much easier and cleaner than my usual methodical approach. I harbor this special gift to attract these types of men. Perhaps going forward I should consider this approach to be my go-to plan of execution. It would save me hours of planning. I enjoyed the point-blank execution; it was hot.

My dearest Listener,

What an enjoyable night I had with my friend. I enjoyed the fuck out of this. I'm starting to realize that I'm a magnet for these cocky, narcissistic males. Not a bad thing, I suppose. It does make me wonder about things in my personal life. Is it possible that Michael is a narcissist and I can't see it? Am I ignoring the toxic traits to keep him in my life? The truth is, I think he is. Over and over I replay various events in my life that point to this scenario.

I literally just pulled the pin in the hand grenade, and with a loud, fiery blast, my life just exploded right before my eyes.

I love him and I'm not willing to let him go, not yet anyway. I have too much to worry about on the outside to think about fixing my own life right now. I'm having fun. Can I be real right now? I'm going to keep doing this. I'm never going to stop until I get caught…

Chapter Fourteen

I feel powerful and liberated. The demons of my sultry side, unleashed and ready to prowl. Michael, my willing servant, accepts all of the benefits related to my darkness. He gives me full control in the bedroom. To date, he has not connected my beastly prowess to the murders of the night. I can feel sweat forming and slowly moving down the small of my back. Flashbacks of my evening with Mario fuel my desires for Michael. I can still taste his blood on my lips, and sharing the taste with my unknowing husband sparks relentless, insatiable sexual energy. I push harder, closing my eyes to relive the game, to smell the panic and fear Mario must have felt as I lifted and pulled the trigger of that gun. I scream in pure pleasure as I gasp to release every ounce of energy I have left in me. Sensing his climax, I tightly wrap my hands around Michael's neck and bring his pleasure to a whole new level. Satisfaction fills my face as he effortlessly lifts me up and gently places me down on the bed beside him. Regardless of my actions outside of this marriage, he is still my soulmate. My ride or die whether we fail or fly. My sexual energy outside of this room doesn't in any way lessen my love or desire for him. It's part of the game, an integral part of the hunt.

Caressing my body, he holds me gently and whispers to me as I'm falling asleep. In and out of consciousness, I try to appear like I'm listening, but I just can't find the strength to fight it anymore. I am out. His whispers, mostly comforting. From the depths of dreamland, I can vaguely remember the things he wanted or felt like he needed to say. Gently rubbing my forehead, he pauses for a brief moment and continues to speak.

"Heather, I know you won't remember this in the morning, but I love you so very much. You are the love of my life. I have fallen short as a man and definitely as a husband. I'm in no place to judge or punish you for any shortcoming. I fear for you. I know things that I wish I didn't know."

His whispers are haunting and I hear every word, at least I think I do. I can no longer fight the need for sleep. I feel the comfort of his hand in mine, and with that comfort, deeply I fall.

The brightness of the sun fades in and out of view as the ceiling fan gently blows the curtain side to side. I roll over and extend my arms around him. He needs to sleep in a little longer this morning due to working the night shift. Even without waking him, I enjoy being near him and feeling the comfort of his heartbeat underneath my hand. I feel small lying next to him. A man of honor, serving his country both as a United States Marine and as a law enforcement officer. How in the world did a man of his integrity get involved with someone like me?

Last night was the first night in a very long time that I was able to sleep through the night. The sins of my past didn't show up to haunt me. Having Michael lying beside me definitely helps. He is my protector, and that brings me comfort. I lean into him and gently kiss his back. Softly, so as to not wake him up, I crawl slowly out of bed and head to the shower. I have a pretty bizarre confession. I have a coffeemaker in my dressing room right next to where I shower. It's genius if you ask me. I have the first cup on board before the shower is even hot.

As I'm washing my hair, memories from the night before start replaying in my mind. Was I dreaming all of this? A slight panic curdles up in my stomach, and I start to feel light-headed. What exactly did Michael mean by his words? Is it possible that he knows? I quickly shake off the feeling. I have to let this go. If I bring it up, it could open up an entire Pandora's box. That could be so much worse! Sometimes things are better left unsaid.

Losing track of time I quickly finish my shower and

dress for the day. I'm meeting Blaze for lunch today, so I have that to look forward to. I haven't seen him since our uncomfortable conversation, and I'm so ready to move past that with him. My desire is to keep seeing him, even at the cost of my relationship with Cassidy. We just have to make absolutely sure that she never finds out. The truth is, I will never leave Michael, so I don't think there is a reason that she would ever need to know. Careful is key here, and I'm the queen of careful. As long as we're honest with each other and he agrees, we are good.

Chapter Fifteen

I'm greeted at work with an awkward silence from Cassidy. Fairly confident that this has nothing to do with Blaze, I find the strength to ask her what's wrong. A deep sigh riddled with desperation segues into a deeper conversation than I expected. A conversation laced with tears and drama.

"Cassidy, calm down a little. I'm having trouble understanding you."

The truth is, I heard every word she said. I'm just not sure exactly how to respond, so I'm trying to stall. The one thing I'm very sure about is that I need to cancel my lunch plans with Blaze. There is absolutely no way I can leave my best friend in the fragile state she's in.

"Heather!" Cassidy exclaims while gasping for air and trying her best to hold her shit together. "I'm a total mess and I need your help! Do you remember the guy from the bar, the bartender the last time we went out? His name was Blaze. Do you remember him?"

"I do remember him. What's going on?"

"Heather, this is bad, it's so bad! I'm pregnant and I'm pretty sure the baby is his!"

"How can you be so sure? Cassidy, you're sleeping with multiple men. How in God's name can you be sure? Calm down a hot minute and let's think this through. Okay, the first question I want to ask is, do you want to have a baby? You have two choices here. If you don't want to have this baby, I will go with you, and we will terminate the pregnancy together. If you want the baby, I think it best to keep your mouth shut and have the baby. Tony will never question the paternity of this child. He's not even going to think twice about it. Either way, I think it best that you keep this between me and you and not another soul!"

Staring out into space, she just sits there emotionless. I grab her hand and sit down in the chair next to her.

"Either way, whatever route you choose, it's going to be okay. I'm here and I will always be here. I've got you, Cassidy!"

Before I could finish my thought, she interrupts and softly she begins to speak.

"I'm keeping my baby. I don't know what this looks like exactly going forward, but I know that I want to keep his child. I will face whatever consequences I have to. Do you think I'm nuts for doing this? What would you do?"

"Well, Cass, we are two very different people. Honestly,

if it were me, I would terminate. But I know how long you've wanted a baby, and I think you will make an amazing mother. You're going to rock this! Take your time and really think things through. Let your heart be your guide; it won't lead you wrong. This too, shall pass."

"Heather, I hope you're right. I'll put a lot of thought into all of this before I finalize my decision. How did I get here?"

Anchored in a sea of critical self-destruction myself, I find it incredibly challenging to offer advice to anyone right now. Especially my best friend. I want to be supportive but at the same time I'm a little salty that this involves Blaze. Instability on both sides has pretty much squelched any possibility of working today. Given the circumstances, apparently so is drinking.

"Cass, I have the perfect idea. Let's close up shop for today and go back to my house and watch old movies and eat delicious snacks. I don't think either one of us is in the mood to sell anything today…even the sunset."

※

That brings a smile to her face. I think this will do us both some good.

"Great idea!" Cassidy exclaims with happiness in her eyes.

THE *Listener*

"The guys will be working late anyway, so we can party all night!"

A surprised look on Heather's face brings the conversation to a screeching halt.

"What do you mean? Did something happen at work?"

"Haven't you heard?" Cassidy responds quickly with a spark of excitement. "Girl, that serial killer hit last night and the night before. Tony told me this morning that it's definitely the work of the same person because the calling card is the same. A heart drawn into the pavement using the blood of the victim!"

I try to appear surprised. "But how? How can they be sure this is the same person and not the work of two different serial killers?"

"Heather, think about it! The police department is keeping this case close to the vest. The calling card was never released in the media, so it has to be the same killer! It has to be! No one else would know about the details surrounding these murders!"

I try really hard to keep a straight face and not react suspiciously. No one would ever suspect me anyway, nor would they suspect that it would be a woman. If my suspicions prove me right, I think the LAPD is falsely reporting the presence of the same calling card. It lessens the possibility to the public that there are two killers out there.

However, in the depths of my mind lies deception.

"I have a great idea, Cassidy. Let's forget all about our problems, forget the pregnancy, forget there is a violent serial killer on the loose; let's pretend that all is right with the world right now. Let's celebrate us tonight. We will chill in our cozy clothes, eat, drink, and be merry! Only, no alcohol for you."

We laugh in agreement, and the night takes a pretty comfortable turn.

Chapter Sixteen

Over the past few months, my relationship with Michael has been significantly stronger. We have always been close, but lately that closeness has been noticeably different. My desire for him has been different. Within me I have found strength and liberation. With that strength, I view our relationship on a different level. I no longer need anyone in my life. Michael is in my life because I want him in my life. I haven't needed him for a very long time.

Being highly respected within the LAPD, he is my camouflage. My coverup for every committed sin. I love him beyond measure, and my lustful desire for him is primal and hot. I want him to be by my side, and with every decision made, a more difficult decision lurks in the balance. Blaze must go! Cassidy announcing her pregnancy complicates things greatly. The risk of us getting caught is no longer worth it to me. My feelings for him are not deeper than my needs right now. I enjoy him but I'm not emotionally committed to him, not yet anyway. There was a time that I was willing to lose both Cassidy and Michael.

Unfortunately, my feelings have significantly changed. I feel like the pregnancy has certainly accelerated that change for me. It's a risk I'm no longer willing to take. I've already earned his trust, so there will be no game in it. I will make it senseless and quick. The urgency is getting heavy, so planning will need to begin. I already know his daily routine. Tomorrow night is my soonest option. When he gets off work at the bar, I will be waiting for him. Until then, I need to put this all out of my mind. He and I have been together long enough that saying I don't feel anything for him would be a lie. It's undeniable that this one is going to hurt, but I feel like I have no other option. My heart will grow numb to it eventually.

With a deep sigh I sit on the side of my bed, place my head in my hands, and cry, inconsolable at this point. My heart, the lifeblood of my existence, feels deeply severed. I'm hemorrhaging. I am flaccid and lifeless. One by one I slip the shoes from my feet and toss them across the room. Weakness and nausea are setting in, so I lie down flat on the bed, still in my clothes, hoping they will pass. My eyes are heavy with exhaustion, and my need for sleep overpowers my fear of closing them. The voices in my head get louder as I drift off, chanting taunting messages as consciousness leaves my body. Suffocating anxiety presses heavily on my chest, making it difficult to breathe. I can't

THE *Listener*

sleep and I can't stay awake. I'm completely paralyzed. To each and every one of the voices, I listen. Sweat is beading up on my forehead, and my eyes are wide open. The angry voices fall silent, yet a single voice remains. My heart starts beating faster, and my eyes surf the room. There are shadows dancing all around me despite total darkness in the room. Cautiously, I sit very still and struggle to listen. Repeatedly, he calls my name. His voice is broken and stressed, and as he starts to speak, I recognize his voice. My heart is quivering and broken, my head shaking side to side.

"No! No! No! .Blaze! What is happening? Tell me who did this to you! Blaze!"

The tears are falling from my eyes, clouding my vision and making the shadows harder to see. With a spark of light filling the room, his voice stops. He leaves as quickly as he came.

"Blaze," I whisper softly to myself over and over. In a fetal position, I roll on my side and close my eyes. I'm crying so hard that I can barely breathe, not that I have the desire to anymore. I didn't realize how much I cared about Blaze until I lost him. The intensity of my anxiety is indicative of my deep emotional connection to him. I will not rest until I find out who is responsible for taking him away from me.

Anxiety-driven exhaustion fuels my immediate need for sleep. As I close my eyes, tears softly fall down my cheek, staining my pillow. With no choice, I fall asleep.

The low rumble of thunder and flashes of light send shadows dancing throughout the room, waking me. With no concept of time, I feel like I have slept for hours. In reality, it was only about forty-five minutes. I feel rested enough, so I crawl out of bed, take a shower, and get dressed for the day. The spark of excitement knowing Michael will be home soon gives me the encouragement needed to get it all done.

I grab another cup of coffee, stretch out on the sofa, and turn on the news. Emotionally charged and filled with anxiety, I pick up the phone and call Michael. On the second ring, he answers.

"Heather, babe, I'm pulling into the driveway now. I'll be in soon."

Nervously, I walk toward the door. The familiar sound of keys clinking together as he opens the door delivers a calm vibe. Michael has always had that effect on me.

"Hey, love." He greets me with a passionate hug.

In the comfort of his arms, I find peace. With every hug, for as long as I can remember, I place my left hand over his heart so that I can feel it beating. Today, it is noticeably different.

THE *Listener*

"Hey, babe, I'm so glad you're home. I missed you!"

A smile lights up his face as he effortlessly picks me up and puts me on the kitchen island, where we spend the next few minutes in silence, passionately kissing. I grab his hands and interlock our fingers. For me, holding hands is a whole different level of passion. With the morning passing quickly, I give him a gentle nudge that I want more. I need him to make love to me. Unapologetically, I wrap my legs firmly around his waist, place my arms around his neck, and whisper in his ear.

"I want you and I need you now. Take me upstairs to our bedroom and remind me why I fell in love with you so many years ago."

"Do I really need to remind you?" he whispers.

My dearest Listener,

It's been a while. We have so much catching up to do. I'm starting to crave the taste of blood. It's time to hunt yet I'm here bleeding on paper to you. I'm broken and I know that Michael and Cassidy are having trouble managing my emotionally charged mood swings. I'm a hot mess and every day brings another layer of chaos. I'm going to cut to the chase.

Blaze is dead, and for the record, I didn't kill him. There is a copycat killer out there using my calling card. There was a heart drawn near his body with his blood. That's my signature and someone out there is screwing with me. It's making me crazy. The truth is, I was going to kill him and it was going to be soon, but they got to him first. My taste for blood has been a raging river as of lately. I have forgone the thrill and safety aspect of the hunt. My desires have shifted more toward an unquenchable thirst and insatiable appetite for destruction. I confess to you tonight that my numbers have more than doubled since we last spoke. Turns out, there are a lot of bad people in this world. I can't get caught until my work here is done. When that time comes, you will help me confess. In the meantime, I'm going to need to change things up a little. I feel like I'm being watched, possibly stalked by this copycat.

While Michael was sleeping the other night, I went through some papers in his briefcase. The police are still claiming that this is the act of one person. Hells bells, is there nothing at the crime scene that sets us apart? I will tell you this: if there's nothing at the scene setting us apart, it can only mean one thing—there's something dark that brings us together. We're both very careful and methodical in assuring the perfect execution. Kudos to them and may the best killer stand the longest.

If this cat killed Blaze, what was the motive? Did they somehow know about our illicit affair? I want to seek revenge, but I also don't want to get caught. I have to let this rest. In the meantime, I will patiently watch.

Confessing to only you as I know that you will keep my secrets safe.

Chapter Seventeen

Rain splashes against the windshield of my car as I sit in silence waiting for a short reprieve. Each drop hits differently, creating a paintball effect that slowly spreads across the window. With every breath I take, a foggy haze clouds my view of the outside world. With a couple of fingers, I reach up and clear the fog away with a small circular motion. Wanting to go unnoticed, I make my view as small as possible. I need just enough to be able to watch. This is no "swipe right" or "lust to trust" victim; he is different, but someone I've had my eye on for a while. A law enforcement officer who has ruined more marriages than he would ever be willing to admit. Classic! I have known of him for a very long time, but now, it's personal. He's an emotionally abusive player and needs to go. My interest in him has sparked something very unexpected, and I think I may be on to something bigger. So for now, I watch and I patiently wait.

"Holy shit!"

I'm startled by someone pounding on my passenger

side window, and struggle to see who it is. Afraid to roll the window down, I just sit there, offering no response. When I peer cautiously out, I can see the silhouette of a tall, muscular, light-skinned man.

"Heather? Open the door. What are you doing just sitting out here alone in the rain?"

Immediately I recognize his voice and unlock the car, inviting him in.

"Andrew! You scared the hell out of me. What the hell?"

We both break out into laughter. True to form, he begins his flirtatious dance in an attempt to seduce me into his web. I'm very familiar with his routine, his every move actually.

"Heather, you look amazing! I saw you a few weeks ago at the bar, and you were dancing with another guy. It wasn't Michael. I admit, I was a little bit jealous!"

He reaches over and touches my hand, twirling his fingers with mine.

"Nothing was going on, Andrew. He's just a friend."

"You mean, 'was' just a friend? He was victim number....hmmmmm. Well hell, I've lost count, but he was one of the victims of Orange County's infamous serial killer. He was brutally shot to death that night in the parking lot of that same bar. Oh, and here's a bizarre twist of fate. I watched you having sex with him moments before. I couldn't help myself. I was horny as shit that night and went out to my car to relieve some pressure when I happened upon quite the show. I busted a load watching you fuck the hell out of him and then you just disappeared into the night and he was never seen again. But don't you worry, Heather, your secret is safe with me. We have a long history of secrets, don't we?"

My heart is beating out of my chest, and I'm sweating profusely. I'm riddled with anger, but I have to handle this gingerly.

"Andrew, there is no secret here. The person you saw wasn't me. I haven't been with anyone else other than you and Michael. Why would I need anyone else in my life? I'm so upset that you're having these thoughts. If you really thought you saw me cheating, why didn't you ask me about it earlier?"

He leans in and starts kissing my neck. The warmth of his breath is incredibly arousing.

"Oh, it was you!" he whispers as he reaches down, unbuttons my jeans, and slips his fingers inside to rub me.

I'm no longer in control of the situation. I want him so badly. A stormy evening and an argument often have this effect on me. He pulls down his jeans and I climb over and sit on top, slowly letting him enter me. Kissing his neck

THE *Listener*

I rock back and forth, slowly and methodically, until he yells out my name and releases in explosive pleasure.

"Choke me," I whisper as I feel my orgasm following his. He grabs my neck tightly and thrusts his hips several times before sending me off into pure, unadulterated pleasure.

Twenty minutes of pure ecstasy, and I'm flooded with emotions from feelings past. Andrew and I have a long history together, and to date, I have told no one. Michael was his partner for several years, which is how we met. From the moment we laid eyes on each other, the sexual energy was off the charts. We have been secretly seeing each other since. Over the years it's been less and less. I had to pull away a bit because I was developing strong feelings for him. The feeling wasn't mutual, and it was becoming painful for me. All he ever wanted was sex, nothing more. The sex was always amazing, so I still desired him, but I would pine for days wanting more. And then there was the real roadblock: he was also married. Well, married may be a stretch. They were mostly roommates, and I don't think she cared at all what he did outside of the home. He also had a long-term girlfriend, which I didn't find out about until a year or more into our relationship. The list goes on.

I knew that he was only using me, but I loved him and I hoped his heart would change.

We say our goodbyes, and I slowly pull out of the parking lot. A light rain gently dances across the windshield. Endorphins still high from my unexpected, pleasure-filled evening fuel a desire to hunt. In the distance the lights of Hollywood Boulevard promise the perfect scenario. Cruising up and down, as I frequently do, I notice a gentleman loitering outside of a mom-and-pop coffee shop. He is in his early thirties, I would guess, but definitely in the prime of his life. My intent tonight was riddled with pure evil, but now I'm feeling very indifferent. I pull up slowly next to him, coasting as I roll down my window to speak.

"Hey, you!" I yell with the full intention of getting his hot ass in my car. "Are you lost? Can I give you a ride somewhere? I live here in Los Angeles, and this isn't the best place for a well-dressed guy like you to be walking at night."

I say this with conviction despite the fact that he is surrounded by impeccably dressed people. With a full display of overly flamboyant confidence, he approaches my car window, leans in, and undresses me with his dark, seductive eyes.

"Hello you too!" Tilting his head to the side and softly licking his lips, he asks, "Did you just summon me?"

It is as if we are old friends reconnecting. It feels so natural exchanging our sexually charged pleasantries.

"I did. Now get in the car! It's not safe out here walking at night."

Without hesitation, he gets in. He turns to me and smiles. The cute dimples on each cheek and the absence of crows' feet give the illusion of youth. Age has never mattered much to me to be completely honest. There is something about him; I just can't put my finger on it. Something vaguely familiar.

"My name is Heather." I quickly offer up an introduction to gain his trust. "I grew up here in Los Angeles, and I am one of the few who never left. I'm a watered-down blend of hippie and accomplished."

I glance over at him to assess his reaction. He's a cutie and I can tell that he is completely enamored with me, making it easier to gain his trust.

"So, tell me, what's your story?"

I glance back and forth, watching the road while hanging on his every word.

"Well, I'm a writer and a wanderer," he eagerly responds.

He looks at me and holds eye contact until I break it. It is in that moment that I feel the intensity of our conversation go up a notch. Maybe even two. I pause and take a shallow breath, waiting for him to continue. He pauses and waits for me to move the conversation forward. He is giving me the illusion of control. This makes me nervous and a little aroused. I've never had a man handle me this way before.

"A writer?" I exclaim with enthusiasm. "I'm impressed, tell me more! What genre do you write? You have my full attention!"

He pauses for a moment and smiles.

"Would you like to continue this conversation over a drink? My name is David by the way. I don't think I formally introduced myself."

I can feel my cheeks starting to blush.

"I would love to get a drink with you, David. I know of a few quiet little places where we could drink and be alone. I'm assuming you want to be alone?"

He smiles and without hesitation confirms his intentions. He points up the street.

"I live in that apartment building, and I have a fully stocked bar. Would you like to go there? It's not much but it's home to me."

He pulls me in once again with those dark, seducing eyes, holding contact until I agree. He reaches into the back pocket of his jeans and pulls out a key card. Holding it between his fingers, he pushes it toward my hands. With

THE *Listener*

a twinkle in his eye and a slight wink, he asks me to pull in, and without hesitation, I do just that.

―⁂―

His apartment is small but inviting. It is dimly lit and I can still smell a lingering scent of men's cologne.

"Make yourself at home, Heather. I will mix us some drinks."

In an attempt to make myself more comfortable, I sit on the edge of the sofa and untie my shoes. Looking up and gazing around the room, struggling to get my shoe off, I notice the strangest thing. David clearly has an obsession with hearts. They are everywhere. Some are on shelves; others are in pictures. I say pictures but they are more like paintings. I'm trying hard not to read deeply into this, but it will be my topic of choice should we find a lull in the conversation.

"Heather, join me in a toast? I don't know about you, but I think tonight was meant to be," he says with a bit of sarcasm. We bring our glasses together, and oddly enough, the evening feels very comfortable. He gets on one end of the couch and I on the other with my legs stretched out and resting comfortably on his. As the night goes on, he rubs my feet and legs, and we engage in one topic after another in an effort to get to know each other. We talk about literally everything. Michael is working all night, so time is not an issue. Bewitching hours are approaching, and David is getting visibly anxious. I can tell he wants more but doesn't know how to progress in that direction. I lean in and kiss him, offering a gentle nudge, and he quickly grows comfortable with my advances. On that sofa we talk for hours, share many laughs, become comfortable with each other, and on that sofa the sun would wake us up the next morning.

"Heather, I can offer you many things here in my humble abode, but coffee isn't one of them. Would you like to offer me a ride and accompany me to the Starbucks down the street?"

He is laughing as he says it, but the seriousness in his voice cannot be ignored. I desperately need some coffee myself, so I quickly accept his offer. As I freshen up and put my shoes on, one of the heart paintings in particular catches my eye. Something about it is hauntingly familiar. He leaves the room, and I quickly snap a photo of it.

"Do you like that painting?"

I gasp and quickly turn around, realizing that he has caught me.

"I do, David. I love it. I's very beautiful. Where did you get it?"

He walks closer and looks at me once again with those eyes, holding contact almost to an uncomfortable level.

"I painted it," He says, still holding eye contact.

"Wow!" I exclaim, while swallowing deeply, a feeling of anxiety starting to overwhelm me. "You're a man of many talents," I say somewhat sarcastically.

Immediately, he rudely interrupts. "Artist! I'm an artist. I write everything that lives within me, and I paint what I can't put into words. Everything that I fear and everything I can't say out loud, I paint! With every stroke of my brush, a story is told, just in a different way."

Panicked by his anger, I quickly put away my phone, hoping he will forget that I snapped a picture. That picture may be my only hope of getting out of here alive. His anger is escalating, and he's moving about the room in hostility, clearly trying to figure out what he's going to do with me. I need to get out of this house somehow, but I have to be careful with my approach. If I can get out, I can get away.

"You know what we need? Coffee. It will give us both a different perspective. I think we have blown this a little bit out of proportion. I didn't mean to make you angry. I love hearts and I am enamored by your talent. They're beautiful and I feel like they each tell a unique story. Would you care to share any with me over coffee?"

He looks at me with glazed eyes and a visibly stressed face.

"Heather, we both know that can't happen. I'm going to need you to sit down and be quiet until I figure out what to do with you."

"What to do with me? David, we both know you don't want to hurt me. Whatever it is that you're hiding, it's not worth hurting me over. I have friends who work with the LAPD, and they likely already know that I didn't come home last night. Trust me, they will be looking for me. Your secrets are safe with me. Believe me when I say that I'm in no place to judge anyone for anything. Let me go and all of this will go away."

Guarding the door and deep in thought, he stares off into the distance.

"Heather, I need you to come with me and I need you to come willingly. I don't want to hurt you and I think you know that. Let me rephrase: I'm not going to hurt you. We need each other right now, so let's stop playing games. We are of one mind and soul. Now, come with me."

He takes me by the hand and walks me down to the basement. I go willingly. I know that if I put up a fight, he will hurt me. It isn't worth that. I just have to trust that I will be okay or he will eventually let me go. What troubles me are his words. What did he mean by "we are of one mind and soul"?

Chapter Eighteen
Michael

Because of his overnight work schedule, several hours pass before Michael realizes that Heather is missing. Tony and Cassidy rush to be by his side as he pleads with police for help. The department is already overwhelmed with months of exhausting investigations and overworked staff desperately trying to catch a serial killer. The dark side of being in law enforcement is the public's assumption that all cops are bad. Michael has been with the LAPD for almost twenty years, his wife goes missing, and he's automatically a suspect.

"Tony, I need your help, man; you know me more than anyone else in this department. You know I would never hurt my wife. Please try to find her. Cassidy must know something! They are keeping me here for questioning, and we are losing valuable time. What if she is the next victim?"

Michael is sweating bullets, and his anger level is rising.

Anxiety is quickly pushing him over the edge, making him appear like more of a suspect. Trying to gain his composure, he wipes the sweat from his forehead. Tony replies while trying to appear calm.

"Cassidy and I will head out now and start looking for her. Try to stay calm, Michael. You know how this looks! They will pin this shit on you if you're not careful. Give me the keys to your house. I need to go in and get Heather's laptop. Have you tried tracking her phone or watch yet?"

"Her phone is dead. I've been trying to send messages for hours, and she hasn't opened a single one of them. She's been missing well over twenty-four hours now, at least I think. It could actually be longer. I worked the overnight shift, and it's not uncommon for her not to be home when I get off work. I went to sleep and woke up around 3:00 p.m., and that's when I realized something was wrong," Michael replies.

Cassidy quickly intercepts the conversation.

"She never came to work yesterday! I have called and called with no response. I'm really worried. This is not like Heather. Something is very wrong!"

As Tony and Cass start walking toward the door, Michael frantically speaks.

"Tony, I need a lawyer. Can you help me find one

that's tight with the DA and send him to me? Please, I need you to do this now!"

"Do you really think you need a lawyer? Man, you've done nothing wrong!"

"Tony! Get me a lawyer! You know how this is going to go. It will not end well for me. I need someone who is going to have my back!"

Hesitantly, Tony agrees.

"I'll take care of it, Michael, and you too. I will never leave your side. I've got your back and we will find her! You have my word!"

As soon as Tony and Cassidy walk out of the office, Cassidy loses it. Tony turns and holds her for a moment.

"Cassidy, is there anything you need to tell me? Do you know anything that will help us find her? Anything? You can't hold anything back if you know something because every minute is critical when someone is missing!"

"Tony, if I knew anything, I would tell you. I have nothing to offer. Heather has not said anything that would be viewed as suspicious. I'm worried about Michael! Why in the hell does he need a lawyer? Do you think he hurt her? Does he have a reason to hurt her?"

"Cassidy, you know cops are always under fire. We are the good guys until they think we're not. Has she ever expressed concern about her relationship with Michael?

He has anger issues, we all do, but I don't think he would ever hurt her. Do you? If you do, Cassidy, you have to tell me. This is not a betrayal of trust; this is life or death for Heather! Has she ever said anything to you to make you think Michael might hurt her or that he would have a reason to hurt her?"

Without hesitation Cassidy insists she knows nothing.

"Let's split up. Cassidy, you go back to work and tear her office upside down. I want her schedule and I need to know the last five homes she has shown. I need her cell phone records, and if she has a laptop there, please bring it home. The Feds will be in soon, and they will take everything. I'm sure they will be focused on Michael, so we can't waste a single moment. Go and get everything you can and meet me back at their house. I'm going to take a quick drive around the city and look for her car. I will meet up with you soon. Please keep your phone charged! Cassidy, I love you. Please don't worry. I will find her or die trying."

<hr />

Everything is starting to get leaked by the media, and Michael is already on trial and viewed as a suspect in the court of public opinion. After hours and hours of questioning, his attorney shuts everything down, refusing for him to answer any further questions.

THE *Listener*

Michael pleads with the district attorney, "I can stay here all night and answer questions, but this isn't going to bring Heather home. I need to go look for her. Our time is critically low. You know yourself that statistically if we don't find someone in the first twenty-four hours of going missing, it usually ends badly. We all know this! Please let me go so that I can help look for my wife!"

The DA agrees to allow Michael to leave with heavy restrictions in place. Walking out of the station is a total shit show. Crowds of people surround them with cameras and microphones, yelling the most absurd things, all blaming Michael for the disappearance of his wife. He is trying hard not to lose his shit as his attorney and two bailiffs help him to the car without being trampled on. As they drive away, Michael looks back at all the people who could be out looking for his wife; instead, they waited patiently to throw stones and accusations at him as he exited the building. *These are the people I have put in hours and hours of overtime protecting. This is the community I have served, and this is how they choose to repay me. Things are about to change, because the moment I step out of this car, I'm taking the law into my own hands. I have to find Heather, and I will do whatever it takes to get her back. I know the good guys, and I know the bad. I have spent my life protecting both. It's time for someone to step up and return the favor!*

Chapter Nineteen

Heather

Most of my days are spent trying to remain calm and sane. An eerie silence dances in the darkness and a dank, musty odor overwhelms the cavernous space that surrounds me. I have no concept of time or even what day it is. I'm free to move about the room, but constant nausea and vertigo are limiting my activity. I think he drugged me for God knows how long until he could figure out exactly what to do with me. I feel like days have passed. I've been watching a bruise as it goes through its natural progression. I can barely see it now, so I'm assuming I've been here for a week, possibly more. He brings food every few hours and for that I'm incredibly thankful, but all I beg for is light. The darkness is making me crazy. I'm in a room with no windows, and I need to feel the warmth of the sun more than I need to eat.

I keep replaying this whole scenario over and over in my head. I just can't figure out how we got here. He seemed like such a normal guy.

I can hear footsteps in the hall, and my anxiety level begins to rise. Sweat profusely beads up on my forehead and cheeks. My breathing is shallow and rapid, and I'm starting to wheeze as I can hear him enter the room.

"Please, David, will you please give me some light," I plead in a desperate and panicked voice. "The darkness is making me crazy. If you want to kill me, just do it! Why do you want to torture me? I really thought you were a cool guy. What the hell happened? I'm not angry with you. I just want to understand what I did to deserve this."

His footsteps are getting closer, but the darkness makes the distance confusing.

"I brought you something, Heather."

He responds better when I'm calm, so I close my eyes and take a long, deep breath. The task seems impossible until a familiar sound changes everything. With a single click, the room fills with light.

"A lamp! You brought me a lamp! Thank you so much, David! Oh my God, you have no idea how much I needed light!"

Tears fill my eyes and uncontrollable emotions take over.

"I know you did," he responds, emotionless.

His eyes are dark and almost trance-like as he gazes all

around the room examining every inch of it as if he had never been in it before. Slowly and methodically he walks all around me.

"You're free to move about the room, Heather. Why are you just sitting here in the corner?" he asks as he stops pacing for a moment, awaiting my answer.

In a shaky voice, I respond, "I'm scared, David." My eyes follow him as he resumes pacing around the room. "Are you going to hurt me?"

He stops but doesn't turn around to face me.

"No, I'm not going to hurt you, my friend. I'm here because I want to save you."

A deafening silence fills the room, and in a lowered, respectful voice I ask, "Save me from what?"

He quickly turns around and offers me an answer.

"I need to save you from yourself, Heather."

He squats down beside me and leans into me, making it easier for him to whisper in my ear.

"I know who you are." He backs away just enough to see the look on my face. He smiles and releases a slight chuckle. "You see, I've been following you for quite some time. Watching your every move, watching you watch me!"

He tilts his head to the side, and his eyes widen as he waits for me to respond.

"Do you hear voices at night, Heather? You know, as you lay your head down to sleep. Do you hear voices? Let me answer that question for you. You absolutely do hear voices. The voices of every victim. They taunt you at night, don't they?"

He gets up and walks slowly across the room. He slides down the concrete wall into a seated position on the floor facing me. Chills cover my entire body, and I start to shiver uncontrollably.

"Are you cold?" he asks.

Ignoring his question, I interrupt in response. "I do hear voices, and I recognize every one of them. They're getting stronger, and the number is increasing almost daily."

I finally look up at him and make eye contact. His eyes are dark with an evil excitement about them.

"I can't stop, David. I never intended for it to progress this way. I was seeking revenge, revenge on bad people. Men mostly, the bad guys who mistreat their wives or girlfriends. I wanted to make the world a better place, but it got into my blood. Now, I crave the hunt and the joy of the kill. I crave the metallic taste of sweet revenge and the smell of fear. I have become a monster. I don't even know who I am anymore!"

I hold eye contact as I wait for his response. His face

completely void of emotion, he just stares at me.

"Are you going to say something, David?"

His entire demeanor changes. "Do you *really* want to stop, and do you *really* have regrets?"

"No and no!" I respond without any hesitation. "I don't want to stop, and I have no regrets!"

He gives me a cold stare and shakes his head in understanding, agreeing with me.

"Heather, does anyone else know? Have you told another living soul?"

"No one else knows. I've been keeping a diary, which will serve as my confession if you kill me. They may have found it already. How long have I been in this room? Without light, I've lost all concept of time."

Without offering an answer he calmly leaves the room, and I'm left alone with my thoughts.

Chapter Twenty

Michael

"Days have passed with no sign of her! Goddamn, Tony, where the hell could she be? Someone has to know something!" Michael slams his fist against the marble countertop.

"Man, you have to calm down!" Tony replies while trying to offer support. "Michael, stay here with Cassidy and me for a while. She isn't working right now anyway since we found out she was pregnant. It will be nice having you here when I go to work. She is terrified of being alone."

"You're having a baby?" Michael asks in a surprised tone.

"A boy, we're having a son!"

Michael grabs Tony's hand and shakes with excitement.

"I'm so happy for you, man! Heather would be so thrilled about this. Did she know?"

Before Tony can respond, Cassidy takes the lead. "She did, she knew the moment I found out. She was with me when I took the test. She was so excited for me. I just can't believe this is all happening right now."

Cassidy breaks down into tears, holding her head between her hands.

"She's coming home, baby. Michael and I will not stop until we find her. I promise you that. I need you to put this all out of your head and take care of you and our baby. Let us do the worrying!"

Tony turns and faces Michael, waiting for him to agree.

"Michael, let's go to your place and gather up some things. Cassidy will go to Mom's house until we get back. I don't want her to be alone right now."

Hesitantly Michael agrees. This is the best plan for everyone's safety.

⚜

Walking into the house is uncomfortable for everyone without Heather there. Every room is dimly lit just as Michael had left it. Heather hated coming home at night and walking into a dark house. Tony paces around the house, patiently waiting for Michael to pack a bag. Then his pace noticeably quickens as he races around checking the windows and doors.

"Michael!" he yells. "Someone has been in the house. Cassidy and I stopped by to pick up Heather's computer the day after you reported her missing. These drawers have been pulled out! All of them! Whoever it was, they were looking for something very specific. Look around and see if you can figure out what is missing. Whoever was in here knew exactly what they were looking for."

Michael takes a good look around. Tony is right. Things do seem to be moved around.

"Michael, go get your phone and check the Ring camera."

A sick and flushed look comes over Michael's face.

"It's been disabled. The last signal I got was more than two days ago."

Tony rubs his head in confusion.

"That bastard has a key to my house! He's been in my freaking house!" Michael yells. "He must have Heather's keys, and he was in here looking for something. We need to call the department and get someone out here to fingerprint! This was no random break-in. This was well planned out, and they were here for a reason! What in the hell could it be?"

Within an hour countless investigators and officers arrive on the scene, working and offering up support. Days of fingerprinting and boxing up potential evidence yield little to no information. No unknown DNA can be found anywhere, further mounting a case against Michael. The husband, especially if he is in law enforcement, is always the first suspect.

I can't afford to waste time being a suspect. I need to find Heather and I need her alive. It's time to take the law into my own hands.

Michael asks Tony not to tell Cassidy about any of this. Nothing good will come out of her knowing that the suspect knows where they live and that he had been in their house. Michael has been put on administrative leave, which angers him, but he can use this time to his advantage. While Tony is at work, Michael will take care of Cassidy. It will give him time to meticulously go through everything, looking for clues. As soon as Tony gets home from work, Michael's work will begin. An undercover vigilante desperately searching for his wife. *I will find her, dead or alive. I will find her and the bastard who took her from me. Los Angeles is a big city, but over the years I have worked every last inch of it. I have made friends and I have made enemies, and I will use both to find her.*

He prints off several pictures of Heather and loads hundreds of pictures from her computer onto his phone. Copious amounts of coffee make his hands shake as he quickly gathers things up. She's in the hands of the heartless serial killer; he just knows it. Ever since Heather has been missing, so has the serial killer. The LAPD dubbed him the heartless killer because of the heart drawing he always leaves, using the blood of his victim. Every heart is the same except for one. To date, he has only killed one female, and the heart he left drawn beside her was a broken heart. Michael would recognize his calling card anywhere. Heather would be his trophy. Imagine the excitement of murdering the wife of the man who has been tirelessly looking for him the past several months. He got hold of a cop's wife. This could be his crown jewel. Michael tried to convince the guys at the station of this, but it fell on deaf ears. It's far less work for them to pin this on Michael than to put additional boots on the ground trying to catch the same man they have failed to catch for the last several months.

Michael uses the cloud to download pictures from Heather's phone. He needs to work fast so he can bolt as soon as Tony gets off work.

With his under armor on and multiple loaded weapons, his journey begins.

Chapter Twenty-One
Heather

I've started briskly walking around the room to get exercise as I can feel my muscle tone melting away. David brings me plenty of food and supplies every day, but I'm not sure of his plans for me. I'm trying to stay optimistic and somewhat strong. It's easier to stay positive now that I have some light. Being in the dark was pure torture, and I don't think I could have done it much longer. Total darkness does very dark things to your mind. I felt like a mad person. Sometimes, it felt like my skin was actually crawling, and I was starting to hallucinate. I felt days if not hours away from death.

I wish I had a pen and paper so that I could write. Although I never really made a career out of it, writing has always been an outlet for me. It's therapeutic and spiritual. It's so ironic, David is also a writer. We have so much in common and he pointed that out to me while we were talking that night. I think about that night constantly.

THE *Listener*

How did I fall so easily into the hands of a serial killer? I think it was my increasing greed and hunger for the hunt. I got lazy and lost focus of my goal. It was never meant to be for sport. I really wanted to rid the world of the evil works of bad people. I always went in with a plan, a plan that I had carefully thought out for weeks and sometimes longer. Somehow, along the way my vision was blurred. It could be so much worse, I suppose.

He lets me take a shower and wash my hair every few days, and it's something I really look forward to. I think everyone would agree that feeling clean always makes you feel better. I don't think he has left the house for days because I can hear footsteps and the constant noise of a television. Since not being able to share my thoughts with my listener, I've started talking to myself, out loud. Sometimes, I convince myself that someone else is in the room. It helps me to feel less alone. It's weirdly therapeutic and it keeps me focused. I think about my diary every day and wonder if the authorities have found it yet. Damn, what if they find that bloody book and then David decides to set me free. That would be my dumb luck. I survive being captured by a serial killer and then I have to spend the rest of my life in prison for being a serial killer. Fuck yeah, that would be my luck. One thing I can't figure out is why he hasn't attempted to rape me. I know the attraction is there because we slept together the first night we met. We couldn't keep our hands off each other, yet somehow I ended up here. He lets me shower, so he knows I'm clean. As a woman, that really messes with my head. Does he find me unattractive now?

I should be thankful that I'm not being abused, but my insecurities are kicking in. I'm talking to myself again and chuckle at how ridiculous my thoughts are. I guess I'm my own listener now.

※

It's almost dinnertime, and I'm getting very hungry. I've started to figure out my days and nights based on my meals and mealtimes. I'm not sure why this is so important to me; it's not like I'm going anywhere, but it does give me an idea of how long I've been here. At lunch I asked him to bring me a pen and some paper. I would be incredibly thankful if he did that as I would rather have that than food. Talking to myself, while extremely therapeutic, gets old quick. That, too, gives me a complex.

I'm starting to get hunger pains, and it feels way past dinnertime. I've waited and waited for my food, and at this point, I've given up. I'm pretty sure it's past my usual time, and for some reason I must not be getting food tonight. Bored out of my head, I grab a cup from the bathroom

THE *Listener*

and fill it with water. The walls are all concrete and I want to draw on them. As a memorial to every life that was lost, I attempt to draw the same heart I left beside the victim. Instead of using blood, I will use water. I know it will only be temporary, but I will enjoy doing it. The concrete is thirsty and absorbent as I finger-paint my feelings onto the wall. It is emotionally charged, but I manage to paint a heart in memory of every life I took. It is the first time that I really want to hear their voices. I want to feel the anger and pain I inflicted. Tears fall from my eyes as I summon them one by one. Still, nothing. No one comes forward. In the middle of all the other hearts, a broken heart for my dear friend Michelle.

I stand back with my cup of water and cry as I stare at the wall.

Chapter Twenty-Two

Michael

All night I have scoured the darkest corners of Los Angeles, showing pictures and talking to anyone willing to talk to me. Not only did everyone deny seeing her, but they also denied knowledge of the serial killer who has been terrorizing LA for more than a year now. Hundreds of lives have been lost, none of them in questionable or dangerous parts of town. That's when it occurs to me that I am looking under the wrong rocks. This is no lowlife freak show or thug and likely not even the average Joe. I am dealing with a highly skilled society person, possibly ex-military or law enforcement—definitely someone with the skills to cover their tracks.

With my newest epiphany on board, I get into my car and drive down to Hollywood Boulevard. I stop at a local Starbucks to get a cup of coffee. While I am waiting for my coffee, I open up my phone and start scrolling through pictures. Heather is such a beautiful woman and I wish I had another chance to tell her that. Over the years I have fallen short both as a man and especially as a husband. I would give anything to have one more chance to be the man I should have been to her all along. As I look at the pictures, my heart is literally breaking. I regret bringing her to LA; hindsight's always 20/20. I've worked in law enforcement long enough to know that the likelihood of us finding her alive at this point is almost zero. I'm not giving up. I won't give up until I find her. God, I need just one more chance to tell her how much I love her. I'm not worthy, but she is.

Visibly emotional, I swallow my pride and continue to scroll when I stumble onto the cloud photos that she took somewhere close to the time she went missing.

"What the fuck!"

My heart is beating so rapidly that I can't catch my breath. I whisper to myself in disbelief, "That's the fucking heart!"

Heather has a picture of a portrait of the heart. The calling card of the heartless serial killer. It is exactly the same. The brush marks of the paint are also similar to that of the blood of the victims. I would recognize it anywhere. Where in the hell did she get this picture? I scroll down to see if there is a location pin marked on the picture, and there it is! This is it! This photo was taken in the last location that she was! Heather, this was a brilliant move! I put the address in my navigation app and drive over to check out the area. To my knowledge, Heather doesn't know anyone on this side of town.

I park the car and set out on foot to get a closer look at the area that was pinned. Unfortunately, it is an apartment building, which really complicates things. It's so much easier to bust into a house than a building with multiple residences. The biggest problem is trying to determine which apartment she is in. I call Tony for help, and with a flash of our badges, we have total access to all of the security footage in the building. For hours we scan the footage. It is getting exhausting. Just when we are going to give up for the night, there it is. Footage of Heather wrapped on the arm of some guy and entering his apartment. She went with him willingly. Clearly, there was no struggle. I feel physically sick. I viewed this with my best friend, and I am completely mortified. With no evidence of a struggle, it will be extremely difficult if not impossible to get SWAT in there. All I can do is sit here and stare at the footage. This cannot possibly be the case. We watch days of footage and never see her leave the apartment. He comes and goes alone multiple times a day, but still, no sign of Heather.

"Tony, I just don't know what to make of this. There's

no way possible that Heather was cheating on me. Not with this guy. I mean, look at him, man. He is so spindly and definitely not her type."

Tony hesitates and I can tell he is trying to proceed with caution.

"I get it, man, but the footage doesn't lie. That's definitely Heather, and she was a willing participant."

"But seriously, Tony, we looked at the footage, man. We never saw her leave. We have to get into that apartment. Heather is in there, I just know she is. The question is, do we go in or do we get the police involved?"

"Dude, if we go in there on our own, that's breaking and entering, We're cops, man, we will get roasted for that! Let's call the cops; we have no other choice. We have to let them do their job! If she's still alive, every step we take is critical. We have to be very careful, and we only have one chance to get it right."

"You're right, man. I'm not thinking straight right now. Let's go down to the station and get the team together. Oh and Tony, I'm going in!"

"What?" Tony exclaims. "Michael, you know that's a really bad idea. You're going to make decisions based on your emotions, and that never ends well. Please, just stay home with Cassidy and let us take care of this for you. Please!"

"Tony, I'm going in to get my wife! Dead or alive!"

Chapter Twenty-Three
Heather

I woke up this morning, and to my surprise I could still see the faint water stains of my heart drawings. The cement was so dry when I started that it soaked up the moisture almost immediately, somehow staining the concrete. I walked up to each heart individually, placed my hand over it, and silently said a prayer. I really enjoyed my water painting activity. I think I will paint some flowers and some type of memorial around it. The funny thing is, while this is emotional for me, I really have no regrets. I would honestly do it all over again, with the exception of Michelle. She didn't deserve any of this.

※

What started out as a flower garden manifests into a huge floral memorial. I add a couple of trees and some wildlife to the scene. As I'm painting with my hands, I'm reminded of what David told me the night we were together. He said he paints what he can't put into words. He paints so that he doesn't have to say it out loud. It's funny, I feel such a strong connection to him. We're both writers and artists of our own disasters. It's frightening really.

Caught up in the moment, I don't hear his footsteps and without any warning, David pushes through the door. I turn around quickly to see him standing there holding a tray of food.

"David, you scared the hell out of me! I usually hear you coming."

He doesn't respond, he just stares at the wall. Without breaking eye contact, he gently places the tray of food onto the floor.

"Heather, this is so beautiful!"

"Thank you, David."

"Tell me about it and please don't leave out a single detail. First, let's get our food out so that we can eat together. I brought enough for us to share. I thought it would be nice to have dinner together."

"David, that is so kind of you. I'm lonely. It's going to be really nice to have some company."

Sitting on the floor facing each other, we break bread while I explain every aspect of my masterpiece. It isn't until now that we have discovered we hadn't copied each other's heart art. It was totally random that they were so similar, almost identical. We both used a heart traced by the blood of the victim to mark as our signature. The unsettling part is how closely they resemble each other. We sit there and talk about it for hours. It's odd how something so dark can bring two people to the light.

"Heather, what can you tell me about your childhood? What do you remember about it?"

He stares at me with his dark eyes burning fear into the depths of my soul. Patiently, he waits for a response.

"Well!" I sigh, knowing that my answer will not satisfy his intention. "I don't remember much, if anything, about my childhood. I have tried to push it all out of my mind. I didn't have a good childhood. I never knew my dad, and my mom was very abusive. By the time I was old enough to drive, I was living on my own. For the lack of a better term, I was homeless. I wanted to know who I was, so I set out to find my dad. That ended up being a huge mistake. He was a narcissistic, abusive asshole, and it didn't take me long to figure that out. My aunt told me that he was always hurting my mom. That struck a memory for me. I can remember him beating her."

I stop talking for a moment to catch my breath and wipe the tears.

"He was also heavily involved with organized crime, or

THE *Listener*

so I was told. David, I think that's how I ended up here. My whole life I have wanted revenge, but a part of me wanted to be like my dad. You know? I wanted to feel like I belonged, like I was part of him. I craved a life of crime!"

I pause and wait for him to answer. Deep in thought, he just offers a creepy, dead stare. Just as I start to talk, he looks at me and places two fingers over my lips.

"Shhhhhhh, did you hear that? I think I hear something upstairs. Footsteps! I hear footsteps!"

Before I have a chance to answer, I hear a man scream in a harsh, angry voice.

"Police! Open the door!"

Neither of us have a chance to respond We are both frozen with fear, and in a few seconds, the room is filled with SWAT. Michael is running toward us, and all I can do is scream.

"Michael! Don't shoot! Don't shoot! Please don't shoot!"

I feel someone lift my body off the ground and throw me up against the wall away from David. Michael fires multiple rounds, and with horrific anger, he kills David.

I just sit there crying hysterically. Michael drops his gun and runs over to me. I know that I have a big decision to make. Nothing that I say is going to bring David back, so my only choice is to protect myself.

"Heather, are you okay?"

He wraps his arms around me, and I lean into him and cry. I hear people upstairs tearing the apartment apart, taking as much evidence as they can get their hands on.

"Heather, I think this bastard is our serial killer. Since you went missing we have had no murders, and you were so smart to lead us here. That picture you took of the painted heart, that is the same heart the killer was using as his calling card. I was desperately trying to find you, so I downloaded your pictures from the cloud, and that picture you took led me here to you! That picture saved your life!"

"Michael, I have no words right now. I don't even know how long I've been here. I want to go home."

"Baby, we have to take you down to the station and get this all processed first. A unit is on the way."

Once the unit arrives, things get very chaotic. They take Michael away first. He is catching some heat for killing David. He never should have been involved with the bust. His actions were purely emotionally charged. David presented no threat to me or anyone else. Shortly after, they come and get me. After hours and hours of questioning, I am mentally and physically exhausted. I don't want

THE *Listener*

to hear all of the details surrounding my disappearance. I lived it, and I don't want to live through it again. Mentally, I'm not stable enough. I can't wrap my head around how I got into this huge mess. I just want to go home, take a shower, and rest. I'm craving the hunt so bad that I can taste it. The warm, metallic cocktail pressed firmly between my lips made sweeter by fear. I want it now! But I need to lie low at least until some of this blows over. Right now, I just want a hot shower and a warm bed. I haven't slept in a bed in so long. I can't say my mind is at peace, but my body needs rest.

※

Shortly after I crawl into bed, Michael finally comes home. Our bodies come together for the first time in a very long time, sending me off into a deep, much-needed sleep.

Chapter Twenty-Four

The morning sun peeks invitingly between the poorly pulled curtains. A cheery invitation for me to start my day. Before my feet even hit the floor, the doorbell rings, and I can hear Michael running to answer it. Quickly, I rush over to my closet to get dressed. Halfway over my head, my rolled-up shirt gets stuck in my ponytail holder and I'm anxiously fighting to get it down. The anxiety of approaching footsteps and a high-pitched squeal of excitement don't help.

"Cassidy!" I yell, excited, as I run helplessly in her direction, still fighting to get my shirt down. "Cassidy, oh my God, you're starting to show!"

Tears of joy fill my eyes as we embrace in a girlfriend hug.

"Heather, girl, I have missed you. We have so much catching up to do. Let's go and get some coffee! Oh, and did Michael tell you yet? The guy they arrested for abducting you, they think he was the serial killer they have been looking for."

I just stare out in a different direction so as to not make eye contact.

"Why do they think that?" I shrug in an attempt to have a neutral look on my face.

Cassidy responds with a puzzled gaze. "Because he confessed! Apparently he left a detailed diary documenting his events. Leaving a trophy trail behind, it was apparent that he wanted the state of California to know who he was. They were suspicious anyway, because the entire time that you were missing, he didn't kill anyone else. That's when they initially suspected it was him."

"What the hell!" I walk over to sit on the edge of the bed. "A diary? Cassidy, you're telling me that he left a diary documenting his crimes?"

Cassidy shakes her head in response.

"Yes, and it documented the details of every single murder and even your capture. He was a sick fuck too! He went into detail about how he would have sex with his victims to lure them into his web. He gained their trust by pretending to be interested in them and then he killed them. Just cold and heartless if you ask me."

"Oh my God, Cassidy, I think I'm going to be sick."

"I know, right! Whoa! If Michael didn't tell you about this, did he talk to you about anything else? Like something way worse?"

An anxious, puzzled look covers my face, and every ounce of homeostasis leaves my body. "Like what? What else was he supposed to tell me?"

Cassidy is shaking her head, alerting a hard no to telling me anything.

"Cassidy, you can't just leave me hanging. Please tell me. I can act oblivious when Michael brings it up! I have to know! Come on and spill the beans!"

I can tell by her body language that she doesn't want to break. I don't want to stress her out, but this is going to make me crazy.

<hr />

We are headed out to the coffee shop to get some much-needed coffee and catch up a little when we run into Michael and Tony doing the same. I can't help but notice a little anxiety and disappointment all over Michael's face as we approach. Papers are scattered all over the table, which they both quickly try to disperse, indicating that they are trying to hide something. Tony, true to form, is genuinely excited to see me. Reaching out his arms, he brings me in for a hug. Immediately, tears fill my eyes.

"Heather, I honestly thought I was never going to see you again. You're a survivor! Welcome home, love!"

I don't want the hug to end. It is a genuine reminder

that I was truly missed. I take a short pause and sigh before I reply.

"Honestly, I didn't think I was going to make it home myself. There were days that went by that I wouldn't even get a glimpse of the sun. I think he purposely did that so that I would lose all concept of time. You rescued me on a good day. He had never actually come into the room and eaten with me or socialized at all before. That was the first time. It was as if he knew something was happening."

"Sit down, ladies!" Tony exclaims as he pulls out chairs and encourages our continued company. I can tell that Michael is riddled with anxiety. I feel certain it has something to do with what Cassidy didn't want to tell me, but I don't want to pressure him. Hopefully, the conversation will segue naturally.

As everyone around me engages in small talk, my mind is wandering in many different directions. While I may appear to be attentive, I honestly have no idea what anyone is talking about. The smell of freshly brewed coffee and the fragrant aroma of the coffee shop are triggering some anxiety for me. Coffee shops used to be my sanctuary, but now they are my hell. Coffee was something David and I shared in common and frequently spoke about. Right now, all I can think about is my diary! I'm literally screaming inside my head. Panic is setting in as I try to avoid showing emotion. Where in the heck is my diary, my trusted Listener? I didn't notice it on my nightstand last night. What if this is what Cassidy was trying to tell me? What if Michael found it and read my diary? Oh dear God, or worse, what if the police found it when they searched the house? So many what if's plague me. I feel flushed and faint; shallow breathing leads to hyperventilation, and that's the last thing I remember.

Chapter Twenty-Five

Distant chatter and laughter startle me as I open my eyes slightly and peer around the room. It is dark, but familiar smells and voices offer warmth and comfort to me. I reach over and turn on a bedside lamp, further confirming that I am home. How did I get here? My body feels sore and weak, and I struggle to even sit up on the side of the bed. The room is spinning, so I sit and wait, hoping the feeling will pass.

"Michael?" I call out as loud as I can, given my weakened state.

"Heather!" he replies. "Baby, I'm here, lying right beside you."

Quickly, I turn around to find that he is resting right next to me.

"Michael, have you been here the whole time? I thought I heard voices, people talking in the kitchen."

A look of concern fills his face.

"No, sweetie, I've been here for hours, alone. You passed out in the coffee shop. Tony and I carried you out and brought you home. Do you remember any of this?"

In a low, monotone voice, I answer him. "No, I don't remember any of it. I barely remember seeing them today."

I can't help myself. I start to cry.

"Am I ever going to feel normal again? I just want things to go back to the way they used to be before all of this started happening. I don't feel like myself anymore. I feel different, almost like I don't recognize who I am. I can barely stand to look at myself in the mirror because I don't know the person who's looking back at me."

Michael tries his best to console me, but the tears just keep coming.

"Heather, we need to talk. This may not be the best time to have this conversation, but I have to get this off my chest. It's eating me up inside."

I feel every ounce of life sink to the pit of my stomach. What could he know? I turn to face him; his chiseled cheeks are red as anxiety fills every blood vessel in his face.

"I'm as ready as I'm ever going to be, Michael. Lay it on me."

Michael pauses in an attempt to gain composure. "Fuck!" he exclaims while running his fingers through his hair and flicking out sweat. "Heather, this is some messed-up shit! He left a diary with a detailed confession. He is confirmed to be the heartless serial killer we have been tracking." His voice lowers as his facial expressions take a more serious turn. "He's a monster, a cold-blooded, calculated killer, and he didn't hold back on a single detail. He was methodical in every approach and the bastard actually saw his actions as vigilante justice."

He pauses for a brief moment, waiting patiently for me to respond. I take a deep breath and try not to freak out.

"Michael, this guy is so evil. Why do you think he let me live? Did he kill Michelle too?"

Michael looks me straight in the eyes. "He did kill Michelle, and Heather, I need you to try to stay calm when I tell you this. I know why he let you live. He wanted to make sure the LAPD knew exactly why he did what he did, including why he spared your life."

I feel numb and stoic. I honestly am not sure I want to know. I can only pray that he didn't share in his portal of thoughts the fact that we had sex. That would be like icing on this whole screwed-up mess.

"Tell me, Michael, please! I need to know! I can handle it. I just may need some time to process things."

Michael takes a deep breath, grabs my hand and looks me in the eyes.

"Heather, David was your brother."

My heart stops and I find myself completely speechless.

Nausea riddles my already weakened state and I started to retch. He gently pulls my hair back and reaches for the trash can. The room starts to spin and weird flashes of light distort my vision. Gently, I slide to the floor and cry.

"Heather, baby, I didn't want to have to tell you this. I think he has been stalking you for a very long time. The diary entries began as far back as five years ago. Maybe more. The investigators have reason to believe that there could possibly be a diary that predates this one."

Realizing now that he gained access to the Listener to protect me, I need to carefully cover my tracks going forward. I still have so much to figure out.

"Where is that diary, Michael? I want to see it. Are you sure about all of this? I mean, anybody can say that they're my brother. Has any of this been positively confirmed with DNA? I want that diary. Where the hell is it?"

I'm really trying to stay calm, but I can tell I'm losing my shit. This is a lot to process right now.

"Baby, the diary is in evidence. I can try to get the DA to show some leniency and allow us to go in and read some of it. I don't think it's a good idea to read it all. It's very dark and extremely gruesome. This guy was spawned from the devil himself, and he spared no details describing his crimes. He took a great deal of pride in his work. I was not even allowed to read all of it. What I read made me sick! As far as confirmation, they took samples at the crime scene and confirmed your relationship. I actually knew it before the investigators read the diary. He's your biological brother, baby. I'm so sorry. If I could change any of this, I would."

"Does it scare you that I'm related to this monster? Have you thought about that? Does this make me a monster too?"

Michael reaches out for me to give me a hug.

"God no, baby, this does not make you a monster at all. You're the most amazing person I've ever known. Do not turn this on yourself!"

Anger is building up inside of me. I need an outlet.

"I want to be alone. Please leave!"

"Heather, no! Please don't shut me out! We can get through this, but we have to stick together. We have to support each other. We have been through too much together to turn back now and this may come as a surprise to you, but I'm hurting too!"

Emotionless, Heather turns her back to Michael.

"I want to be alone, Michael. I'm sorry but please leave!"

CHAPTER TWENTY-SIX

Cold chills travel from one end of my body to the other. Just the thought of sharing DNA with David creeps me out. Clearly, that's why he asked me about my childhood and what I remembered of it. He was trying to figure out if I remembered him or not. My childhood was never good, but never in a million years did I expect anything like this. I'm having a lot of trouble processing it all. Is it possible that he knew our father? I vaguely remember him mentioning in conversation that his dad died in prison. If this is true, I need to know why. This is all starting to make sense to me now. I never really had a stable home. I was tossed from pillow to post most of my young life. I never felt wanted by any of the family that ever took me in. They all took me in out of obligation or the fact that they were getting paid to take care of me. I was grateful to have a place to stay, but it never felt like home to me. I guess I never really knew what home was supposed to feel like. If David was my brother, why have I never seen him and why did he have sex with me? He is sick in the head. Sadly I'm trying to justify why he did it. He must've had a reason, something dark that I won't immediately understand. Hopefully, someday this will all make sense.

I don't remember anything about my mom or dad other than the fact that they were never around. My childhood is a complete blur, and nothing that I remember about my teen years is good. I never really fit in, and every day was a struggle. My name changed multiple times; my uncle said it was for my own protection but never offered a deeper explanation. I was always expected to accept everything and question nothing. I never grew comfortable with my life. I just grew numb.

During my sophomore year of high school, I fell into the hands of a few goth girls. As bad as that may have seemed, those girls saved my life. I felt like I finally belonged, like I was wanted. My hair was already black, and my wardrobe from head to toe was black. My entire life was void of color and I loved it. I finally fit in. Aside from the occasional dabbling in witchcraft, we were a pretty good group. Even considering the gothic phase and the witchcraft, nothing I recall in my childhood can explain the person I have become. How did I go from a shy gothic girl to a heartless killer? I need to get my hands on that diary. I feel like David left these answers in there. He certainly did a good job with the Listener, although I'm not sure if he just embellished his own diary with information I had written in mine or if he rewrote it all. Either way, this was all very fortuitous for him. Somehow, he saw this coming and planned well for it. I just have to figure out how to get to it all.

Pieces of the puzzle that is now my life are slowly and methodically starting to come together. Until I get all of this straight in my head, my mind won't rest. I keep hitting rewind on every conversation that David and I had. If I gather enough pieces, I hope to connect the dots and get some sense of direction. Despite the negativity and questions surrounding this whole scenario, I still need closure. Every day, I tell everyone that I'm okay, but I'm definitely not okay, and I don't think I will ever be okay again.

On the bed I've laid a simple black dress. David would have loved this dress. It's a simple design with a lot of secret messages sewn into it. I designed it myself and had it made a few years ago. Every hem is sewn with red thread instead of black. The red thread is a symbol of my hidden sorrow as I look at my victims in their final resting state. The lining of the dress, also in red, symbolizes the fear they must have felt as they lay gasping and holding on to their last few seconds of life. A single heart-shaped red button for each victim is sewn underneath the collar and added as necessary. These are my trophies as they keep count of every life sacrificed to make the world a better place. Every detail of the dress represents something significant to each victim. I have never missed the memorial of any of them, as it is important to me that I pay respect to each and every one of them as they are laid to rest. It's my final gift to them. The last but most important detail are the red gloves, which signify the blood on my hands. This is how I express my empathy, the only way I know how. Now, I must go and pay respect to my only brother.

With a sick and nervous stomach, I get dressed and prepare to leave the house. I stop at a neighborhood florist and pick up a single red rose to place discreetly inside the coffin. While I didn't know at the time that he was my brother, I still feel a strong connection to him.

The parlor is full of people. David was obviously known and loved by many. None of whom I'm sure suspected that he was a serial killer. It holds a little less stigma when you're charged after death, I suppose. Into the casket I gaze as tears fall down my face. I'm numb and emotionally exhausted. People are starting to line up behind me as the pressure intensifies for me to walk away. I place the single red rose on his chest and silently whisper my last "I love you," and slowly I walk away.

"Excuse me! Excuse me!"

A tall, bald gentleman, impeccably dressed in an Armani suit, is desperately trying to get the attention of someone. Not realizing that his anxious request is directed at me, I continue to head to the door.

"Excuse me, Miss, is your name Heather?"

"Yes, yes it is," I reply nervously.

"This is for you. I'm sorry for your loss."

Standing over six feet tall, the gentleman hands me a black letter-sized envelope. It feels like a book and I'm a little apprehensive to accept it. With a puzzled look, I kindly thank him and walk away. Tears are starting to blur my already sensitive eyes as I subconsciously accept the fact that what's in this envelope could possibly change my life forever.

With the envelope clutched tightly in my hand, I begin my journey home. A leisurely walk is not in the forecast as the sky is growing dim and the low roar of thunder suggests a change of plan. I pick up the pace and struggle to stay focused in an effort to make it home faster. The last thing I want to do is to call Michael for a ride. I'm in no place to see anyone right now, especially him. I need space and time to sort this all out. Just as I approach the front door, the storm rolls in with intense fury. My body is tired

THE *Listener*

and all I want to do right now is sleep. I desperately need sleep.

To ensure my ongoing solitude, I gather up a few essential items and move into a guest room. This will not thrill Michael, but at this point I have no other choice. I'm a mess and no one deserves the emotional hell that is me right now. The anger I have built up inside of me as a result of David's death is immeasurable, and because of that, I'm afraid to be alone with him. I know Michael was only protecting me, but that doesn't lessen the anger I'm feeling. Right now, my bed is calling and everything else will have to wait. I ease my body into the bed and sink comfortably underneath the blankets. I sigh with relief as I can feel the weight of the world drift slowly off my shoulders. For a brief moment, I gaze up at the ceiling and lose myself in thought. My eyes are heavy, and my body is settling in for a deep sleep.

The wind is ferociously blowing, and the low roar of thunder breaks the silence in the room. Subconsciously, I'm aware, but the depth of my sleep is barely broken. Slowly, I shift my head from side to side. My eyes shoot open and look straight ahead as I hear someone whisper my name.

"Heather."

I gasp and lift my head to look around to find no one

there. This was not just any voice. It was David.

With excitement and fear in my voice, I respond, "David? Is that you?"

I sit up in bed. Carefully, I listen, seeking out any other voices. There is nothing.

"David, please don't leave me. I'm not angry, I just want answers."

Patiently, I wait, pleading for him to come back. I peer all around the room, looking for some sort of sign. In our last conversation, he spoke of voices and signs, and while I'm very familiar with hearing the voices of my victims, I don't recall any signs. What could he mean? As soon as that thought hits my mind, a loud bang startles me. Out of breath and feeling like a panic attack is coming on, I slowly get out of bed and cautiously look around the room. Oh my God, there it is. There's my sign! I run over and on the floor in front of the dressing table is the envelope that the gentleman handed me at the memorial service. It just randomly fell to the floor. This is my sign! David wants me to open this envelope before he speaks. I sit down on the floor with my legs crossed over each heel, holding the envelope in my hand. I pause for a brief moment to gather a few thoughts, take a deep breath, and rip it open. Inside is a letter that he had written and a black hardback journal. Eager to see what he has to say, I anxiously open the letter.

My dearest sister Heather,

If you're reading this, one of two things has happened. They have either captured me or killed me. Either way, I must pass the torch to you. I can only imagine how difficult this must be for you as you are just finding out about my existence. As for me, I've known about and followed you for many years. We are of the same soul and mind as our father, and his father, and possibly many more. We have designer DNA or to put it bluntly, DNA designed to kill. Only, we consider ourselves the good guys, craving the taste of blood while masquerading our sins as vigilante justice. We are passionate and methodical in our mission, and we carry it out with pride. I will continue to be here for you just as our father was for me. For the times when you feel lost or without direction, I will be your compass. Call out to me and trust the process. Inside the envelope along with this letter you will find a black journal. That journal is your Bible going forward. Everything you need to know is inside that journal, including a detailed master plan. Your life has been chaotic the past week, and I feel confident that you're already craving the hunt. Read and study this journal as it is your new life guide. I love you and until the day you need me, I will live silently within your soul.

Love, David

THE *Listener*

Reading this letter is extremely surreal. I feel so connected to him somehow. How can I have a connection with someone this strong that I don't even really know? I guess I never realized or thought about how much our DNA impacts who we really are. Clearly, it does. I'm feeling the weight of the world on my shoulders right now as the legacy of my bloodline is all on me. I know I can do this. I've *been* doing this, but I need to do some soul searching and return to my roots. Along the way I've lost sight of why I started this journey in the first place. What started as vigilante justice and an effort to make the world a better place has culminated into a thirst for blood. For me to continue progress on the mission, I need to let things cool down a little bit. I need to make things right with Michael. As long as our life is in turmoil, he's always going to be suspicious of something. I could really use someone to talk to right now. I miss my diary. I miss having a listener, someone to confide my deepest sins to without fear of judgment. I'm just not sure it would be safe to do so again. In the past before all of this came to light, I wanted to confess. I wanted the world to know who I was and why I did what I did. Things have changed and I feel justified in my actions, and now I want the legacy to die with me.

CHAPTER TWENTY-SEVEN

I feel energized and determined for my day to go well. Going back to work is going to feel weird and a little uncomfortable. For thirteen days I was confined to solitude in a basement with very little human contact. I was driving myself mad being alone, but now that I'm out, I feel weirdly uncomfortable around people, and I really don't know why. Thirteen days is a long time to be alone, but during that time I was never hurt or abused. I guess the seclusion made me feel insecure with the outside world.

As I approach the office I'm greeted by a smile that could illuminate the night sky. Cassidy eagerly opens the door and brings me in for a hug.

"Heather! It's so good to see you this morning. I bet it feels amazing to be back to work. We have two showings scheduled today in Malibu. Should we Nobu after?"

Before answering, I walk over to my desk, take a seat, and gaze around the room. I didn't really expect anything to have changed; it just feels nice to be in a familiar space.

"Is that coffee I smell? I'm going to go with yes on

Nobu, but first, I need coffee!"

"Heather, you know I made it extra bold just for you. I'll grab us a cup; you stay put and just relax. Oh, and a package came for you this morning. It's on the edge of my desk if you want to open it. It looks personal. Maybe it's a gift from someone?"

I can't help but notice the sarcastic little chuckle that follows. Cassidy always has such a vivacious sense of humor. My curiosity is piqued, so I make my way over to her desk to open the package. The first thing I notice is that it doesn't appear to have been mailed and there is no sender name. For a brief moment, I hold the package in my hand and contemplate whether or not to open it in front of Cassidy. Unfortunately, my curiosity is stronger than my anxiety, so I proceed to open the box. Chills and tingling rapidly develop up and down my arms.

Not realizing that Cassidy is approaching with our coffee, I whisper as I gasp quietly in shock. "These are the signs you spoke of."

"What signs? Here's your coffee. What are you talking about? Signs?"

With sweat forming on my furrowed brow, I pull out a journal from the box. It is beautifully designed with what appears to be a colorful hand-painted tree on the front. It is a light shade of blue and appears purposely a little blurred. The branches are heavy with leaves and lightly scattered with moss. It is beautiful and will be a perfect place to share my thoughts.

"Cassidy, did you see who dropped the package off? There are no postal markings anywhere on the box. Was it delivered this morning?"

"Yes, it was delivered shortly after I arrived this morning. A tall gentleman dropped it off. He was wearing a long coat that was buttoned up, making it difficult to see what he was wearing underneath. He was also wearing a hat. Honestly, he came and went so quickly that I didn't have time to think about looking at him. I couldn't even tell you what color his hair was or if he had hair at all. I think you're reading too deep into this. It's just a gift that someone obviously wanted you to have. No harm, no foul, right? Now, finish your coffee and let's go sell a house."

Cassidy is right, there's no harm done here. This is a manifestation of everything David warned me about. Well, warned may be a strong word. Informed would be a better choice. He told me that not only did he hear voices, but he also experienced visions and signs. All of which are starting to happen since he passed away. This morning after reading his letter, I questioned whether or not it was a good idea for me to continue confiding in the listener. I put it out there and this is how the answer was brought to me. It is a clear message confirming that it is okay.

"You're absolutely right, Cassidy, no harm, no foul! Thank you for helping me not overthink this. Let me grab my purse and we can head out. Hey, did you think to tell the guys to meet us for dinner tonight?"

"Actually, I did and they're both going to meet us after work. We will go there a little bit early, grab a table, and have a cocktail and a mock-tail. I thought it would be nice for us to have a drink and catch up a little bit before they arrive. I miss you and there's so much I want to tell you."

I take a second to gather my thoughts before asking Cassidy the question whose answer I'm not sure I want to know.

"Speaking of things we need to talk about, how are things going with you and Tony? The last time we spoke, you told me that he had been a real asshole to you. I was shocked because I've never seen that side of him. How are things going now, and have they gotten any better since the pregnancy?"

Judging by the look on her face, nothing has changed. Hopefully, it has not gotten any worse. I'm almost afraid to know. With hesitation, she replies, "Let's continue this conversation tonight, if that's okay. I think it would be too deep to cover in the short time we have."

Knowing that she is right, I agree.

It feels incredibly invigorating to be fluffing pillows and talking shop again! Malibu is one of my favorite places on earth. Not to mention the income possibilities here. Property is expensive and easy to sell. Even with the serial killer off the streets, Cassie and I still enjoy working together. We are the sunset dream team of Malibu, and there isn't a house that we can't sell! We just have that vibe about us! Tonight, we're holding an open house in one of the most exclusive parts of Malibu. Celebrities galore attend, and within the first two hours of the showing, we usually have several offers. Multiple offers is the best-case scenario for us as it ignites bidding wars among the buyers. Bidding wars often guarantee multiple digits over asking price. A win-win for everyone.

Cassidy can't drink tonight, but I have no shame indulging without her. In fact, it has become a necessary tonic in our recent conversations. The unavoidable topic of narcissism and bad behavior being displayed by the man who is supposed to love and protect her. The same man I've known for years, or thought I knew. Clearly, you never really know someone. I have tried to suppress the negative thoughts in my head about Tony. The last thing

THE *Listener*

I want to do is hurt Cassidy and that beautiful baby who is on the way.

A cocktail and mock-tail toast is on the way and the anticipation is high. We have so much to cover tonight. Frosted martini glasses with a sweet, frosty delight await our cheer. We bring them together for the first time in weeks, toasting the life we have going forward and everything we're leaving behind.

"Cheers to new beginnings!" Cassidy shouts as we enter a whole new phase in our conversation. "Heather, I'm so glad you're back. For a minute, I wasn't sure that this night would ever come. I'm really thankful it did. I cannot imagine facing this new journey into motherhood without you. You asked about Tony earlier. Honestly, it's not good. It hasn't been for years, but it seems so much worse since I got pregnant. He is so mentally and verbally abusive that I can hardly stand to be around him anymore. It's just painful and our intimacy is almost nonexistent. He's only joining us tonight because he knows you guys will be here. I don't really want to be with him anymore, but at this point, what am I going to do? I have no desire to be a single mother. I wish things were different but I just don't know how to change them. I'm not stupid. I know I let him get away with treating me like this for way too long. I used to love him and that's why I stayed, but it's getting harder and harder to justify staying. Having this baby doesn't make things easier. I'm terrified of how my life is going to look in the next few years."

Cassidy is not holding back her feelings tonight, and she's not painting Tony in a very positive light. I don't want to respond with anger, but I don't like where this is headed. I need to proceed with caution.

"Do you know for sure that the baby is his?"

Cassidy replies with little hesitation.

"Blaze is the father."

Immediately I feel sick and angry. Trying hard not to show emotion, I pretend to be distracted by conversations going on around me. I know that if I don't look at her, I won't tear up and cry. The silence is deafening, and it is becoming obvious that I am avoiding a response. I make eye contact with her and bring my nearly empty glass to my lips to take a long sip that will hopefully put me on a road to courage. Just as I get the courage to spew a response, Cassidy glances over my shoulder and a smile lights up her face.

"Heather, the guys are here!"

A sense of relief floods my body, and with no time to react, I jump up and reach out to greet them both with a hug. The waitress sends over additional drinks, and our night with the guys is off to an awesome start.

THE *Listener*

For the next two hours we fill the room with joyful banter and laughter. It is surreal. Part of me is totally present, and part of me is sitting in the background observing this magical moment. It is just like old times, back in the day when we were carefree and still very much in love. With all of our underlying secrets, I don't feel like things will ever be the same. Life is unfortunately that way sometimes, and we just have to roll with it. Tonight is a gentle reminder of how fragile life really is and how quickly it can change. We're all in this together, and hopefully we can stay that way.

The drinks continue to flow until the lights go off. It is one of the best nights of my life.

My dearest Listener,

My friend, it's been a while and I've missed you. I wasn't sure if I was going to ever be able to talk with you again. So much has happened since we last spoke, but I will have to fill you in on that later. I'm exhausted and ready to get some sleep, if I can get some sleep. First, I need to vent and share my feelings. Recently, Cassidy shared some very disturbing information with me. She admitted that the baby isn't Tony's. She also told me that Tony has been abusive to her both mentally and physically. She claims it has actually gotten worse since the pregnancy. She also used the term "narcissistic." We both know what this means… However, only one of us knows why this could be a problem for me to carry out.

My confession to you tonight… A few years back, I started having an affair with Tony. I use the word "started" because it never really ended. He's Michael's best friend and my best friend's husband. We have always been careful not to allow our feelings to show outside of the bedroom, but lately it's been really hard. When he hugged me in the

THE *Listener*

coffee shop the other day, we just melted into each other's arms. How am I going to handle this? He's an asshole to his wife, and I should be able to take care of things, but I love him. I don't know if I'm in love with him, but I do love him enough to want to protect him from me. What should I do? I've never been here before. He's always been so good to me… I can't lose sight of the mission. I speak these words out loud. I need guidance from David.

My eyes are heavy so for now, I must try to sleep. Thank you for listening, my friend.

Chapter Twenty-Eight

I sigh with relief as my body slides comfortably between the sheets of my warm, inviting bed. Soon, Michael will be joining me, and to avoid any thoughts of passion, I'm going to go to sleep. He's drunk anyway and he knows that I need to rest. As I close my eyes tonight, I'm reminded of how thankful I am for everything that has happened. As traumatic as it may have seemed at the time, it's been life-changing. Finally, I know where I came from and who I am. With my eyes wide open, I take a deep breath, look up at the ceiling, and softly whisper, "David, my dear brother. I need your guidance tonight. I can feel you all around me, so I know that you know the situation I'm in. Please help me, as I am lost in the mission."

The wind is unforgiving as it harshly blows between the aging cracks of the windowsill. Eerie sounds dance around the room, mingling and peacefully coexisting with the darkness. Exhausted and unable to sleep, I lie motionless, peering around the room and listening to the sounds of the night. Waiting and wondering if I will hear voices or receive a message. A short time later Michael crawls into bed.

"Michael?" I whisper.

"I'm here, baby. Are you all right?"

"I'm okay. I just can't sleep. My mind is going in a million different directions. The funny thing is, I don't really feel tired, so I think I'm going to just get up and start my day."

Michael rolls over and wraps his arms around me lovingly.

"Heather, you're going to get through this, but it's going to take time. In the meantime, you need to rest. When was the last time you got a good night's sleep? I'm not sure that you have since you've been home, and I know you didn't sleep well there. Cuddle with me and just rest. I really want to hold you close to me right now. Let me get you some sleepy time tea. Would that help you fall asleep?"

Reluctantly, I take Michael up on his offer. Sleepy time tea may just do the trick. If nothing else, it should help me relax a little. I roll over onto my back and try to relax. The wind is howling, and a tree branch is brushing up against the window, making an intermittent high-pitched, scratchy sound. For most, this would be annoying, but I really enjoy it. The low whistle of the wind is comforting to me. My eyes are starting to get heavy while I wait for my tea. As I close them and start to doze off, an unfamiliar sound startles me. My eyes shoot open, but I don't want to move. I wait to hear it again. It sounded like something fell into the bathroom sink, but I can't be sure without getting up to check. Slowly, I get out of bed and walk over to the bathroom door, push it open, and take a quick look inside. I run my hand up the side of the wall to find the light and turn it on. I gasp with horror as I look up and see something written on the mirror. Startled, I look around the bathroom, and no one is there. I quickly reach underneath the sink and grab a bottle of Windex and a towel. I have to get this off before Michael comes back with my tea. As I wipe, the color just smears across the mirror. Lying in the sink is my favorite lipstick tube, and it is ruined. As I wipe the last blur from the glass, Michael softly taps on the bathroom door.

"Heather, is everything okay? I have your tea. Heather?"

"I'll be right out, babes. I had to go to the bathroom. I'm finishing up now."

I quickly put away the cleaning supplies and wash my hands. Who knew that a short, simple name like "Joe" could make such a mess. Joe. Who the hell is Joe, anyway?

Trying to appear refreshed, I pull myself together and slowly open the door. As I reach up to turn off the light, I

THE *Listener*

glance back in confusion at the mirror before heading over to the bed. Michael has perfectly placed several pillows on my side that allow me to sit up comfortably and drink my sleepy time tea. Before I can finish, he drifts off to sleep, leaving me awake with my thoughts. I don't know anyone named Joe, not that I can think of anyway. I will remain vigilant while I wait for other signs.

My eyes are getting heavy. I lean into Michael and softly kiss his cheek. Finally, I feel like I could drift off. I push my head into the pillow and pull the covers up to my chest. A quiet chuckle accompanies my humorous thoughts as I whisper softly, "David, the next time you leave me a sign in the form of a note, please don't use my favorite lipstick!"

With my sense of humor engaged, I drift off to what I hope will be a place of rest.

Chapter Twenty-Nine

My office in Malibu is beautifully located between two other office buildings that directly face the ocean. Although I have no plans to show homes today, I came in simply to enjoy the sounds and smells of being on the water. The constant barking of the sea lions used to be annoying to me, but I have grown to love it. With my second cup of coffee in hand, I scoot down comfortably into my chair and prop my feet onto the desk. The morning has been peaceful but it's drifting away. Alone with my thoughts I pull out my diary and refer to the Bible pages. David told me that everything I needed to know going forward would be referenced in these pages. I'm hungry and I need to hunt. Enough time has passed, and with a few changes, I should be able to move forward with the mission. I will have to make some minor changes to my calling card, and that will be a game time decision. I have to thumb through this book and see if I can find any clues That will lead me to who the hell this Joe person is. The deeper and more focused I get into the book, the more I realize that this isn't so much a

THE *Listener*

direct read as it is a passage of riddles methodically thought out and written in such a way to buy time. Clearly, he didn't want me to rush into my next steps. I have lived in Malibu for many years and I know this area very well. David keeps mentioning Upper Edge Brew. There isn't a place I can think of that comes close to this name. Brew can be slang for coffee or beer. Upper Edge, damn! I can't think of anything this could be code for. I pull out a local city map of restaurants, bars, and local pubs to see if I can figure out what exactly he is referring to.

"Upper Edge Brew," I whisper quietly as I peer out at the sunset. "David, I need another sign, a better clue. I need direction!"

Almost immediately after I send a plea to David, my little black book of clues falls to the floor and slides across the room. A little piece of paper floats gently into the air and lands on the floor beside it. I quickly grab what appears to be a gum wrapper with a handwritten message on it. Excited to see what is written, I open it to the words "upper education."

"Upper education, upper education?" I repeat to myself as I scratch my head, trying to figure this all out. "Joe Brew. I've got it! I've got it figured out!" I say out loud with confidence. Upper education is Pepperdine University. That's it! He must be referring to the coffee shop that's at the top of the hill. Now, I must go there and figure out who this Joe is. I'm wondering if Joe is the name of my next victim or if Joe is going to be the clue that will lead me to the place. Joe, as in coffee. I'm loving the suspense and excitement of putting this puzzle together. "I'm ready to do this!" I exclaim as I grab my purse and head out the door.

***

Pepperdine University is just a short drive from the office. It's been a hot minute since I've been on campus, but I know there is a fairly large coffee shop at the top of the hill. It's just a matter of finding it again. As I approach the top, I start seeing signs that say coffee shop ahead, so I know I'm on the right track. The view from up here is so amazing. It's a bird's-eye view of the unforgiving waters of the Pacific Ocean. The colors that are chasing the sunset are nothing short of magnificent. I finally reach the top of the hill and immediately see the parking lot for a coffee shop. A large wooden illuminated sign beckons me. Upper Edge Brew Haus.

"This is it!".

Pulling into a space directly in front of the entrance door, I peer inside and see a gentleman who seems oddly familiar to me. I decide to sit inside the car and wait for a few minutes before entering the building. Fortunately, with darkness upon us accompanied by the bright lights of the coffee shop, it is easy to observe what is going on inside. The barista is young with long, light-colored hair. From a distance, she appears to be pregnant. Intensely watching what's happening inside, I fail to notice the parking lot around me. My car is the only car parked out front. Nervous that I will be noticed, I move the car to an adjacent parking area and walk over just close enough to see what is going on inside. I squat down in some shrubbery and continue watching and observing their every move. The body language of the man is oddly familiar to me. My patience pays off and I have intense butterflies in my stomach as the gentleman starts hugging the barista with what appears to be deep emotion. He kisses her forehead as he turns around and approaches the door. I grab my cell phone and open the camera app to take a photograph. This is no Joe. Joe is a fucking clue. A good one too. This is my next victim all right, but his name isn't Joe. I gasp in disgust and anger as I whisper, "Fuck you, Tony!" You're next, my friend.

I wait for several minutes until I see his car exit the parking lot before walking over to my car. I'm letting my anger get the best of me, but I have to be smart about the planning process. Tony is a significant part of my life, and I have to be very careful about how I execute this. I don't think I can point-blank kill him without letting feelings get involved and end up in a more dangerous situation. I can't make love to him and expect to find the strength to kill him after.

❧

Aimlessly and without direction I stare out of the window of the car. The lights in the coffee shop turn off, and I expect that his lover will walk out at any moment. This may be my only opportunity to get a better look at her. I start the car and slowly drive into the main parking lot pretending that I'm turning around. She's so damn young. What the fuck, Tony. I lean into the windshield to get a closer look. I definitely think she's pregnant. A closer look yields a small but very defined baby bump. Knowing this will make my job somewhat easier. I hate the thought of him abusing Cassidy while she's pregnant and treating this young lady like some kind of goddess. He disgusts me.

❧

Driving home the reflexes in my throat are in high gear, giving me wicked cottonmouth. I'm thirsty, but not just for water. I need blood. The taste of blood fuels my passion to kill, and right now I'm feeling dehydrated. I need the metallic taste of sweet revenge dancing on my tongue.

THE *Listener*

In the distance, just at the bottom of the hill, I can see the neon lights of a gas station. Slowly I pull into a parking space just in front of the door. The clerk, a middle-aged gentleman, is completely enamored with something he's watching on television. I walk in completely unnoticed and help myself to a fountain drink. With very little attention paid to me, the cashier rings up my order and I pay. As I'm walking toward the door, a weird feeling comes over me, as if someone else is in control of my body and actions. I turn around and shout over to him.

"Hey, what are you watching that's so interesting?"

With a big smile on his face, he returns a quick reply.

"*In the Line of Duty*. It's so good. Have you ever seen it?"

Without answering, I turn around and walk out the door. I can hear him yell as I'm leaving.

"*In the Line of Duty*! Don't forget it. It's a really good show!"

That is my sign. I need to off Tony in the line of duty. It's the cleanest and easiest way.

I learned two very important things tonight. The signs will always come if I'm open to receiving them, and David is somehow working through me.

Chapter Thirty

Days have passed and I can feel the pressure building up. While the concept of "in the line of duty" seems like a slam dunk, it's going to be extremely complicated. These days, cops rarely patrol alone anymore, and every time they pull over a car for any reason, they call for backup. Tony and Michael are partners, so I have to be very careful planning and executing this. I don't want another situation like I had when I killed Michelle. I will never get over that. I think I would turn the gun on myself before I hurt another innocent bystander. Especially if that person is Michael. I could never hurt him.

⁓

I've been following Tony for days and tracking his every move. His routine doesn't change much. He goes to the range, the gym, and typically home. He hasn't been on patrol for a while, and I'm not really sure why. I may have to schedule a night of intimacy so that I can get the scoop on his schedule. It's been a while since we've met up. I have to assume it's because he has a much younger side hustle now. I'm low priority thanks to her. Tony and I have been having an affair for a while now, and despite how much he's getting on the side, he will never say no to me. Our chemistry is primal and hot.

The morning is slowly drifting away, and I need to fuel up on some coffee. I was too rushed this morning to get any, and my head feels like it's splitting open. With that thought comes the low roar of my phone vibrating. I flip it over to see who it is. *Well, speak of the devil*, I think before answering.

"Hello, baby." I try to sound sexy as I answer.

"Heather, it's been way too long since we spoke, and I just needed to hear your voice. How have you been?"

"I miss you, Tony, that's how I've been. I need your touch, my love. I need to feel you inside of me. Can we meet up soon?"

I'm sitting in the parking lot of the range and looking right at his truck.

"How about right now?" he asks.

"Are you working? Michael left early this morning, and he said that you guys were on patrol together today. What's going on, Tony?"

He sighs and I can tell that he is hesitant to answer.

"Yeah, that was a lie. I would rather meet up and talk

in person. Are you busy right now? Can you meet me somewhere?"

"I can, but now I'm super paranoid. If you're not working, then where the hell is Michael? He told me he was at work with you!"

"I'll answer all of your questions later. Meet me at The Mill and I will head on over and get us a room. I'm horny as hell anyway, so this is a win-win for me. I will text you when I get in and send the room number. Is that cool with you?"

I pause before answering but I know I have to go.

"I'll be there, Tony! See you soon."

I'm not in the room for two minutes before I melt into his arms. Our chemistry is so strong when we're together. He's passionate in every move, and his attention to detail cannot be compared to anyone I've ever been with. I think we're in love, and deep down, we both know it.

⚜

In the heat of passion I grab the bottom of his shirt and gently pull it over his head. He's kissing me passionately as I rub my hands up and down the muscles on his arms. His body is a work of art, a masterpiece that he spares no expense perfecting. He gently lifts me up and lays me down on the bed. My body is shaking with excitement as he slowly undresses me and goes down for a pleasurable taste. I deeply sigh as I feel a release of stress that I have needed for a very long time. Softly, I call his name and summon him up to me. With the weight of his body upon me, he pulls my hands up above my head. He's passionately holding his hands in mine as he pushes his love deeply inside of me. A tear drifts slowly down my cheek as reality is hitting me hard. I can't kill this man. I love him too much. I have for a very long time, but I've tried to suppress my feelings for the sake of our families. I've never even told him how much I love him. My heart is hurting so bad right now.

He makes eye contact with a beautiful smile attached.

"Babe, that was so good for me." He doesn't even notice my tears.

"Tony," I sigh in response. "That was incredibly amazing. I've needed this for a very long time."

We both get up and get dressed but continue holding each other while in deep conversation. With his back against the headboard and my back against his chest, I am seated comfortably between his legs. His arms are folded tightly around me. It is just like old times. I know the conversation is about to get deep, but I wouldn't trade this moment for anything in the world.

"Tony, spill it! What's going on with you and Michael? What's with all the lies about work?"

He pauses long enough to make it concerning. I spin around in the bed to face him, breaking our interlocked hands.

"Tony, what the fuck is going on?"

"Heather, don't freak out when I tell you this. You have to promise me that before I tell you anything."

Riddled with fear and emotionally charged anger, I agree while trying to appear calm.

"Michael and I got suspended. We are both on a paid leave of absence until the investigation is over. It's highly likely that we will both be fired. Please don't repeat any of this to Michael and definitely not to Cassidy. She will freaking flip out!"

My heart is pounding out of my chest as he's waiting patiently for me to respond.

"Oh my God, Tony. Why? What has happened that it warranted you both being suspended? What did the two of you do? Does it have anything to do with Michael shooting David when I was rescued?"

"Well, it has to do with David, but it has nothing to do with Michael shooting him."

"What does it have to do with then? Stop playing games with me, Tony, and tell me the damn truth!"

"It has to do with you! That's why I'm hesitant to tell you!"

THE *Listener*

I can't help but notice a little escalation in Tony's voice.

"Me? What about me?" I ask.

"Heather, Michael knew long before all of this shit went down."

"He knew what?" I scream.

"He knew about David, and he knew that he was your brother. He has known for a while and so have I. We also knew that he was the serial killer. One of them anyway."

"What the fuck do you mean by that, Tony? What are you trying to say?"

"I'm saying that we know everything, Heather. Don't play me for a fool! We knew and we have tried to cover all of this shit up to protect you! We did it for you, Heather! Michael didn't want the world to know that David was your brother, and he certainly didn't want them to know everything else."

At this point, I'm having trouble breathing. I'm so upset.

"Oh my God, Tony! That's what he meant!"

"Meant by what? What are you talking about?"

"A few months ago, Michael and I were talking in bed, and he thought I fell asleep. He started whispering things to me. I'm not sure if he wanted me to hear them or not, and I was afraid to respond."

"Heather, what did he say exactly?"

"He said he knew things that he wished he didn't know. He also said he was afraid for me. Tony, I think I'm going to be sick."

"Why did you pretend not to hear that? That's some deep shit right there!"

I pause briefly before responding.

"What else does he know?"

Tony hesitates again, but this time he refuses to answer me.

"All you need to know is that we did this all for you. We took the fall to protect you, and we both love you, Heather. Did you hear me?"

He grabs my chin and gently pulls my face toward him.

"I'm in love with you, Heather. I don't care what you have done, and I don't care who your brother is. I love you and I will do anything to protect you. I want us to be together. We can get through all of this!"

Not sure how to respond, I just sit there staring at him. I feel like I want to cry, but the tears just won't come.

"Heather, please say something." His voice is escalating. "Say something!"

"What do you want me to say, Tony? I love you too. I have for a very long time, but we can never be together. This is all we will ever have. You know that!"

THE *Listener*

"Why?" he shouts. "Why can't we be together? We've been doing this for so many years now. Hasn't it meant anything to you?"

"What about Michael and Cassidy? What about them?" Now it's my voice escalating in anger. "You have a baby on the way! Well, at least you think you do!"

I jump up out of the bed, grab my clothes, and proceed to get dressed.

"What the hell does that mean? I think I do? What the fuck, Heather? What do you mean by that?"

I stop dead in my tracks and look him straight in the eye.

"Stop right there, Heather!" He holds his hand slightly out from his angry face. "Let me save you from the extreme guilt you're going to feel later. I know it's not my baby. I got a vasectomy years ago. I had to do it. I knew deep down that I never wanted children with Cassidy or anyone else if I'm honest."

The silence in the room is deafening. I just stand there and stare at him.

"Tony, why? Why would you do that? What if I wanted a baby with you? Were we seeing each other when you made the decision to do this?"

He replies quickly.

"We were not seeing each other. Cassidy and I had just

gotten married when I decided to do it. She has no idea to this day. Every time she brings up wanting a family, I just shut it down with discouragement. Heather, I have a daughter."

He lowers his head and pauses.

"How old is she?" I ask in a broken voice.

"She's twenty now and lives here in Malibu. Please don't judge me. I was fooling around unprotected, and her mother got pregnant. She never really wanted me to have a relationship with the baby, and she never asked me for money. I chose to be part of her life way back then, and I'm still very much a part of it now. I wouldn't trade it for the world. She's pregnant right now and I'm going to be a grandfather."

I let out a deep, shocked sigh.

"She works at the coffee shop on the hill, doesn't she? I saw you with her."

"Yes, that's her. After I found out that her mother was pregnant, and knowing deep down that I would never be faithful to anyone, I made the decision to get fixed. I know this is shocking and hurtful to you, but you deserve to know the truth. That being said, I knew that Cassidy's baby wasn't mine, and I have no desire to know who the father is."

"Well, he's dead!" I say out loud before thinking it

THE *Listener*

through. Literally, I am saved by the bell. Tony's phone rings and he walks away to answer it. I would like to hope that he didn't hear what I said, but I'm pretty sure that's impossible. I head over to the bathroom to take a shower. Hopefully by the time he gets off the phone, our last conversation will be a distant memory.

I pull back the shower curtain, reach in, and turn on the shower. While I am waiting for the temperature to rise, I turn around and face the mirror. With both hands resting on the vanity, I hang my head in confusion. I need strength. I don't even know who to pray to anymore. Tony is not the bad person I thought he was. That was his daughter, and while I'm not happy about the situation, I do understand. David made it very clear that Tony was to be my next victim. Finally, after all these years of wanting to be together, the stars are lining up, but the universe is stacked against us.

Carefully, I step into the steamy hot shower and stand there letting the water run over my body. It feels so good. I grab the soap and start lathering up when I am startled by Tony yelling something through the door.

"Hey, babe, I've got to run. I love you and I will call you later."

I can tell that he is standing on the other side of that door, waiting for my response. For the first time ever, I reply, "I love you too, Tony. Thank you for an amazing evening. I look forward to seeing you again."

With those words, I hear him walk away. I have wanted for so long to tell him that I am in love with him. I've waited even longer for him to say it back.

I rush out of the bathroom and quickly get dressed. Darkness has fallen and the parking lot is dimly lit. My footsteps echo and the only thing I can hear are the heels of my shoes as they tap against the pavement. A lesser person might have been fearful. I fear nothing but the darkness in my own head.

As I approach my car a flashing light from another vehicle that is parked very close to mine catches my attention. Suspicious that this is no coincidence, I continue to walk past my car to check it out. The closer I get to the car, the more anxious I become. I approach from the rear, hoping to go undetected. Reaching into my purse I pull out my 45 and quietly slide in the clip. I can feel that he senses my presence. I can smell the fear. I quickly scan the car to confirm that he is alone. I need and desperately want to watch every ounce of blood leave his body. Gently, I tap on the window and give the illusion of a damsel in distress. Effortlessly, he walks right into my trap. His body is delicious and I picture myself having sex with him. Before I can finish my thought, I pull out the gun, point it directly at him, and

THE *Listener*

pull the trigger. The look on his face is a diluted combination of shock and fear. I didn't hit the sweet spot, so I get into his car so that I can watch him die. I open the glove box, and a shiny object catches my eye. It is a Swiss-made pocket knife. An excited smile rocks my face as I straddle my tiny body around his waist. Feeling him against me is arousing as I push my pelvis against his and treat myself to the third orgasm of the night. I open the knife, lay it firmly against his neck, and pull it across. My lips go in and my tongue tastes what is left of his soul. With blood still on my lips, I kiss his cheek, leaving behind my DNA. This will be my new calling card. A sloppy, unplanned kill. To date, the LAPD hasn't tracked me yet, and I've left plenty behind. Still, I've gone unnoticed.

My insatiable appetite for both of my desires tonight have been fulfilled. Yet I still have a longing to hunt. Michael is expecting me home, so I need to tame my desires and return to him.

※

With blood spatter on my face and lips stained with guilt, true to form, Michael greets me with no questions asked. After weeks of wondering, I now know what he meant that night when he whispered those words while I was sleeping. He knew way back then that I was a monster, and he lives to protect me. He loves me that much. Cleaning up scenes and erasing my DNA, slowly, I'm dragging him to hell with me. He is the epitome of unconditional love.

"Heather, let's run you a bath, my love, and get you to bed. You must be exhausted, and it looks like I'm going to need to go back to work. Tell me where you were tonight, baby."

I pin my location and send it to him in a text.

"Thank you, babes. I'm exhausted. A hot bath and an inviting bed sound amazing right now."

With a kiss, I send him off. Sinking my body into the tub, I call out to David, pleading with him to help me change my direction. After several minutes of no response, my mind begins to wander. Deep down I knew that Tony would go with Michael tonight. They always stick together. Ride or die, they are loyal to each other. Michael would be crushed if he knew the truth. Loyalty over love, is there really such a thing?

Clean and tucked away in my soft, warm bed, I close my eyes in hopes of sleep. Hopefully, when I wake up tomorrow morning, this will all be a distant memory.

Just as I close my eyes and settle in to sleep, I gasp with fear as I awake to the sound of a child saying the Lord's Prayer.

THE *Listener*

"Now I lay me down to sleep, I pray the Lord my soul to keep. If I should die before I wake, I pray the Lord my soul to take."

"Did you hear that?"

I gasp in fear again and turn my head quickly to see who or what was speaking to me. Barely able to breathe, I respond, "Who's there?"

"That's you, Heather, praying as a child, knowing that your words would go unheard."

With tears falling down my face, I reply, "I remember. I desperately needed someone to save me, even back then. I knew of the evil that lived within me. I could feel it. Yet, no one came to save me. No one cared enough. Not even God, or at least that's how I felt. I still say that same prayer every night, and it continues to fall on deaf ears."

"It's too late for you, Heather. You have already been summoned. You were born with DNA designed to kill, and there's no turning back. It already lives within you."

"There has to be a way," I softly whisper. "There must be a way to break this generational curse!"

"There is no way!" he shouts. "You belong to me now. With every beat of your heart, my blood flows within you!"

Anger fills my body, and I clench my fists until my hands bleed.

"There is a way! David, I know this is you. I can break the cycle, and it can end with me!"

Silence fills the room, and his presence leaves as abruptly as it came.

"God, please help me," I pray. "I don't want this monster living inside of me anymore." Over and over I whisper the Lord's Prayer. Still, I feel no sense of peace.

Chapter Thirty-One

Tony

Loud banging on the door of Tony's house sends his dogs into an angry rage.

"I'm coming!" he shouts as he cautiously approaches the door. "Who is it?"

"It's me, man, let me in. I need your help!" Michael responds in a panic-stricken voice.

Quickly Tony pulls open the door. "What's up, man? You look like hell. Are you okay?"

"Get dressed, Tony. I need your help. Heather hit again and we need to work quickly."

Knowing that Heather has been with him most of the evening, he hesitantly replies, "What? Are you sure?"

"Fuck yeah, I'm sure. Get dressed and let's go. We have to work quickly!"

Tony grabs his coat and heads out the door with Michael.

"Where exactly are we headed?" Tony asks.

"She pinned her location here in a text. Put this into your navigation and see how far away we are."

As Tony plugs in the location, he asks, "The Mill! Are you sure this is right?"

"Yes, I'm sure! She told me to look in the parking lot on the north side of the building."

Knowing that this is the exact location where he and Heather were parked earlier, Tony starts to feel anxious.

"There!" Michael shouts as he pulls into a nearby parking space. "Look at the driver's side window. It's partially broken; this has to be it."

Michael puts the car in park and kills the lights. They both arm up and head to the car for a closer look.

"Oh fuck," Michael whispers. "Fuck! Fuck! Fuck! This is the private investigator I hired to follow Heather. She must have somehow known or found out about it. Oh my God! Grab that camera, Tony! Gather up all of his belongings, get everything out of the car, and then help me get him into the passenger side seat. We need to get him to a different location fast! Preferably one without cameras!"

Anxiously, Tony replies, "What the fuck, Michael! Why did you hire a private investigator to follow Heather?"

"Tony! We can talk about this later. Right now let's get him moved to a different location. Go to the other side and pull him as I push him over. We need to get him over so that one of us can drive the car."

Tony hesitates for a moment, grabs the man's arm, and pulls him over. Blood is smeared across the seat, and the metallic smell is getting overwhelming. The driver's side is riddled with clots of blood spatter, and thick, viscous blood is in the floorboard. Rigor mortis is just starting to appear, indicating that he has been dead for at least two hours. Meaning, Heather had to kill him when she left the hotel room. She must have caught him taking photos or a video. *There is a definite possibility that he photographed me as well,* Tony thinks, starting to feel sick.

"Dude, I think this is far enough. I'll drive," Tony says sheepishly.

"I hear you, buddy, let's roll!" Michael replies. "Let's drive him up to Old McCade's Farm. It could take days if not weeks to find him out there."

About thirty miles out of town, Tony and Michael deliver the crime scene to the farm and quickly head back to town. Knowing that Tony is riddled with questions, Michael proceeds to explain the need for the private investigator. Quickly, the conversation segues into a deeper problem. The possibility of Tony being somewhere on one of those cameras.

"Tony, to answer your question about the private investigator, I have felt for a few years now that Heather was having an affair. Over the past several months, it has become more and more of a possibility. She's happier when she's not with me. That's painful for me to admit. Bro, we haven't had good sex in weeks. She doesn't even look at me the same. I have to know who it is, and it looks like my answers may come tonight."

"Have you ever stepped out?" Tony quickly replies. "Seriously, have you? It's not the end of the world if she's having an affair."

"Never! I've never stepped out on her. The only other person I've been with since we've been together was Lisa, and that was Heather's idea. For my thirtieth birthday she invited her into our bed for a threesome. That was the only time, one and done!"

"Dude!" Tony chuckles. "You're one lucky man."

Michael shakes the private investigator's camera in the air. "Remind me of how lucky I am after I look at this camera. I'm afraid my luck is about to change."

"Man, do you really want to look at those pictures? Everybody makes mistakes; none of us are perfect. Heather has been through a lot, and this is going to hit her hard. Deep down, do you really want to know? Do you suspect it's someone you know?"

"Tony, I don't think it's just one person. Several of the crime scenes that we have bleached had trace evidence of semen. Look at the guy we just dumped. Did you not notice that his pants were unzipped? I'm pretty sure she's had sex with most if not all of her victims. I realize that I can't classify her victims as an affair, but I would still like to know."

A look of concern fills Tony's face.

"What the fuck, man. That's sick as hell. Are you sure? Why in the hell would she do that?"

"I'm very sure, and to answer your other question, yes, I do suspect she has been having an affair with someone I know. I think she's been actively doing both. I just feel it in my gut, and I'm usually right when I get that feeling. I'm going to sit on these tapes for a few days. I don't want to overreact. I need to mentally prepare myself before I unleash the truth."

"Michael, slow down!" Tony exclaims while looking out the windshield of the car. "Look! What the hell is going on up ahead?"

Blue and red lights from multiple police cars are coming from every direction. On foot, a tall, light-skinned man is running with multiple officers in pursuit.

"They're chasing that thug. We have to help! Quick, turn the car around and get as close to him as you can. I will jump out of the car and jump him!"

Michael hits the brakes, turns the car around, and goes

full force toward the assailant. Tony jumps out of the car and body slams the guy to the ground.

"Tony!" Michael screams as he approaches the two with at least five other officers surrounding them. Overwhelmed by adrenaline, gunshots and bullets fill the air around them from behind.

"Officers down! Officers down!" another officer screams. "Hold fire! Hold fire!"

Law enforcement officers are everywhere. Running toward the scene with his gun engaged, another officer yells, "Call an ambulance! Two officers and the assailant have been shot multiple times. It's Michael and Tony! Get an ambulance here now!"

The scene is chaotic, proving the perfect scenario…

Methodically, into the darkness I walk, wearing my Louboutin heels, a black hoodie, and red lipstick.

DNA designed to kill… The legacy lives on…